Teenage assassin

Nolan Jones

Contents

Chapter 1. New school

Joey POV

It was a new day, new time and new start. I'm joey smith and my life isn't what it seems. I have no family, just me in a large house.

I don't have any family because my parents died when I was three and I was put into an orphanage.

A couple adopted me but they sold me off to get a lot of money. All my life I have been beaten, shouted at and put out into the world.

At age 13 I was put on the streets with nothing but a phone and the only clothes that were on my back.

The men that took me trained me to become the best of the best and to kill. They told me that different gangs would call me when they needed someone to do their dirty work.

One day, that phone rang. I picked it up to only be told a location and time to be there. And only one name that has stuck with me forever.

At the end, I came out with enough money to buy myself a small apartment in sunny California. During the last five years, I've made more and more money.

The only thing about me is that I'm well known. Well my name, people are scared and try to stay on gang leaders good sides.

I've done a good job to hide my identity so no one can get me. At least they could try. Being in Los Angeles keeps me busy, with all the gangs I get a lot of work and a lot of money.

For me to kill one person will make me around $1 million. Good for me as I don't really need to do anything, I just sit on top of buildings and kill any threat towards gang leaders.

It's not all that bad, but that's how I've grown up to be. It's all I've ever known. To keep myself in the dark and to kill any threats.

Well that's my life story, and now, I get to go to school. I'm joey Smith, I'm 18 years old and an assassin. This is my life.

~~~~~~~~~~~~~~~~~~~~~~~~~

I walk through the gates of the school with my bag on my shoulder and book weighing it down.

"Excuse me. Can you tell me where the office is? I'm new here so I don't know." I asked a blonde girl who obviously bleached it.

"Ugh." She rolled her eyes. "Down the hall to the left."

"Thanks." I muttered then walked in the direction.

As I walking down the hall, I was stopped by a girl with bright blue hair. Her smile made me smile a little as well.

"Hi, you must be new, I've never seen you here before. I'm Lauren." She stuck out her hand.

"Joey." I shook her hand.

"It's nice to meet you. Welcome to ridgeback high. You'll fit in fine here." Lauren had the biggest smile on her face.

"Nice to meet you to."

"Shitzles. I have to go but I'll find you at lunch. Bye joey." Lauren hugged me then walked off.

I shook my head and carried on making my way to the office.

"Hello, how can I help you?" A middle aged woman at the desk smiled at me. She had grey hair and stunning brown eyes.

"Uh I'm new. I'm joey Smith." I told her.

"Of course. Here's your timetable and locker number with the combination. Have a good day." She smiled at me giving me the paper.

I took what I needed and left the office. The halls were now filled with students. Most were talking, some were on their phones and others were having full on make out sessions.

I eventually found my locker, only to see the same blonde from earlier with a guy making out right in front of my locker.

"Excuse me." I called out. They both ignored me so I said it a bit louder.

After five minutes, I got annoyed and spoke up. "Hey blondie, move so I can get to my locker." I shouted.

She pulled away from the guy only to look at me like I was a disease. Well, I'm sure she's had more than one but who's to judge.

"Can't you see I'm busy?" She scoffed.

"Can't you see I need to get to my locker but you and dipshit there are in the way."

"Go somewhere else then. We're busy."

"This is my locker now move or I'll make you." I gritted my teeth.

"Whatever." She flipped her hair and walked away. The guy followed her like a lost puppy.

"Fresh meat. What's your name sweetheart?" A voice said behind me. I turned around to see two blondes with blue eyes and a dark brown haired guy with light brown eyes.

All three very attractive but I could tell they were stuck up their own asses. They were all well built as well. I could only imagine them to be in some sort of gang.

"Joey." I said bluntly.

"Well sweetheart, that is a lie. What is your real name?" The brunette came closer to me.

"My real name doesn't concern you. All you need to know is that people call me joey and that is how it'll stay." I spat out at him.

"That's not very nice is it? We've been nothing but nice to you. No need for the attitude." One of the blondes smirked.

"Leave her alone Grayson. And you two, just stay away from her." I heard Lauren.

"Well isn't it little stone. Come here baby." The brunette smirked at her.

"I'm not your baby and never will be. Now leave my friend alone."

"What are you gonna do little stone. You can barely hit a bean bag." He rolled his eyes.

"Shut up Grayson. You know how Abbott is, now leave her alone before I show you what I can do." Lauren glared at him.

"Listen here you little bi-,"

"What are you going to say?" A deep voice said.

There was a 6'3 guy stood there. He had dark brown hair with red streaks. His piercing blue eyes glared at the brunette.

"Not much boss. Maybe you should control this little cousin of yours."

"I don't need to do shit. Now shut up and get to class like the good little boy you are. Same goes for your two. Now go."

The three boys all replied with 'yes boss' and left.

"You both alright?" The same deep voice asked.

"Yeah, just that dipshit never knows when to stop. Thanks Abbott." Lauren hugged him.

"And you?" He turned to me.

"I can look out for myself, but thanks." I kept my face neutral and no emotion in my eyes.

"Good. I'll see you later Lauren, make sure you keep away from Grayson." The guy told her then left.

They must be close. I thought.

Chapter 2. New friend

Joey POV

As I was walking to my first lesson, I was listening to Lauren talk about how much she loves her boyfriend.

"Have you ever had sex joey?" Lauren blurted out.

"Uh no. I'm a virgin. I've got a lot of work to do so I don't have time for all that stuff." I told her.

"What! We are going out clubbing Friday night and you my honey, are going to get laid."

"I've got work. I don't know what time I'll be finished."

"Where do you work? Maybe I could keep you company."

"Uh no. It's a not the usual job. I've got to be alone but I'll ask my boss to see when I finish." I told her.

"What are you some gang member or something?" She snorted.

"What?! No, it's just that I don't like people knowing where I work. How about I give you a ride to my place Friday then you can stay and wait for me. Invite anyone you want." I turned to her.

"Totally. That sounds like fun. Is there anything you want me to bring?"

"No. I'll get what you want. I'll give you my number and then you can message me the drinks and what you want. But I have one condition."

"What may that be?"

"Don't wonder. I'll put you and your Friends in a big enough room with a tv and shit. Just don't explore my house?" I begged.

"Ok. That sounds fair since you are letting me have a mini party. Thank you and I promise to keep my end of the deal." Lauren squealed.

"No problem. But if I find out anyone went through my stuff, it won't end that well." I joked.

"You   sound   like   my   grandpa."   She   laughed.
~~~~~~~~~~~~~~~~~~~~~~~~~~~~

The day went by really quickly. Me and Lauren exchanged numbers and she messaged me what she wanted for drinks and food.

I got in my black Ferrari and went to the liquor store.

When I got there, I was welcomed by the owner, Miguel. He took me in off the streets when I was younger so he knows all about me.

"Ah, there's my little assassin. How are you?" Miguel hugged me and kissed both my cheeks.

"I'm good, how are you?"

"Well I've missed you around. I've been good besides that." Miguel smiled.

"I've missed being here. But you can always stay with me, you know I have more than enough room in that huge house of mine." I laughed a little.

"I still don't know why you chose that house Bonita. It's so big but only you in it."

"With all that money, I just don't know what to do with it. That way I can get rid of it and still have enough room for me." I shrugged.

"I know. What can I do for you anyway?"

"I need some alcohol. I've got some friends over on Friday for drinks and that. But I have a job to do first so I need to keep them entertained while I'm gone." I told him.

"Of course. Pick anything you want. It's on me." Miguel smiled.

"I won't be drinking because of the job. So I'm paying. And if you don't take it I'll tell Gloria." I giggled.

"Fine. Next time, let me treat you and your new friends." Miguel told me seriously.

"Si Miguel." I laughed. I looked at the list Lauren sent me and I got all the drinks. I ended up getting three bottles of each alcohol. Jack Daniels, bourbon, Smirnoff vodka, Hennessy and Bacardi.

"Thanks Miguel. I'll come by and see Gloria and the kids. Adios." I waved at him after I payed.

"Adios my little assassin." He called after me. I laughed as I walked out of the store.

I put the liquor in my car then went over to Walmart to get snacks. I got, jolly ranchers, Pringles, lays, Hershey's, m&ms, butter fingers and Oreos.

When I was done, I took all the bags back to my car and went home. I had a nice beach house which was cosy, but it was huge and lonely with just me.

It wasn't all bad, but it was very lonely when I was there. Most of my time was taken up by my job and school so it didn't really bother me. Only if I had roommates, eh, screw that. I have many spare room full of weapons so I don't need people knowing what I look like as well as my job.

When I got home and put all the bags on the island in the kitchen, my phone started ringing.

"Hello?" I answered.

"Is this joey Smith?" A man asked.

"This is she."

"Ok. I have a job for you to do. I need Alexander Johnson killed. He is trying to take my gang, weapons and drugs. Can you do that?"

"Of course I can. How much?"

"$2 million." He said.

"Consider it done. Text me when and where and he won't see tomorrow morning." I told him and hung up.

'Port is Los Angeles. 11:53pm. I'll be there with the money after.' A text message came through.

After I read it, I shut off my phone then went up to my room to get dressed. I changed into black jeans, a black T-shirt with a long black coat. I paired it with my usual combat boots and my signature dark blue bandana covering my mouth and nose.

I went into my weapons room and got my sniper in a bag then headed to the LA docks.

When I pulled up, I hid round a corner and set up my gun. Once I was ready, I saw my target and got ready for the kill.

I let out a breath then pulled the trigger. All my guns has silencers on them so I can get around easier.

"Smiths here. Move out." One man shouted. The man that called me, chuckled at the dead body and looked in my direction.

I came out from my hiding spot and went over to get my money.

"Nice work Smith. Maybe I should have you come work for me permanently. You never let me down." He smiled darkly.

"You know I work alone. Now give me my money." I glared at him. He gave me a thick envelope and I looked inside.

"If it's not all there I'll kill you. So pay up if it's not."

"I never let you down. Since you do such a good job for me, I always return it. Farewell miss smith. Expect a call from me next week." He wiggled his fingers then walked away.

I got back to my house and showered. I changed into some shorts and a tank then climbed into bed. Damn long day.

Chapter 3. Friday night

Joey POV

It was now Friday, thank the lord up high. But I was having Lauren and her friends round. Good thing I didn't touch any of the food and drinks since I had no idea how many people Lauren invited.

"So are we still able to go to yours tonight?" Lauren came up behind me.

"Yeah totally. I'll be leaving at 9 and coming back around 11 or 12. So you can do whatever, music, pool, drink. Just remember, no wondering." I told her.

"Of course. I'll keep my end of the deal. I just need to know your address so I can text the others."

"Yeah." I told her my address and she pulled out her phone. "How many people will be there anyway?" I asked.

"Six of us. Is that ok?"

"Sure. Yeah just tell them my rules and we won't have any problems." I laughed a little.

"Perfect. See you later. I'll meet you outside after school." Lauren hugged me then ran off.~~~~~~~~~~~~~~~~~~~~~~~~~~~~~~~

"Are you ready?" I walked up to Lauren.

"Hells yeah. I've been waiting all week. The others are coming around 6." She replied.

"Fine by me." I shrugged.

We got to my car and Lauren's eyes were wide and her mouth wide open.

"This is yours?" She looked at it.

"Uh yeah. I have another at home and a dark blue Porsche." I laughed nervously.

"How rich are your parents?" Lauren asked while we got in.

"I don't have any. My parents died when I was three. I've been moved around most of my life. I was taken in by a store owner when I was 13. A little while after that I left." I told her.

"I'm sorry joey. I didn't know you went through all that."

"I've been through worse. But that's a story for another time." I laughed then took off.

"How the hell did you afford this? Who the hell are you?" Lauren gasped when she saw my house.

"It's not much, but it's home. It's always open so stop by whenever you want." We both walked up to the door.

"I don't have a car. My mom and dad don't have that much money in the family." Lauren's eyes glossed over and she looked down.

"Come with me." I went inside and took her to my garage.

"Are these all yours?" Lauren gaped at all my cars.

"Yes. Now which one do you like the most?" I looked at her.

"Uh. Has to be that white one." She pointed to a white Aston Martin.

"Here. It's a gift. From one friend to another." I handed her the keys.

"No I can't joey. I can't accept this." Lauren shook her head.

"Please. That way you can go anywhere you want. And if you need to get away for a while, you have some way for getting here."

"I don't know how to thank you." She let a few tears slide.

"It's ok. I have this many, what's one less gonna do?" I laughed.

"Thank you so much." Lauren hugged me. We went back inside and I showed Lauren where she can and can't go.

At six, the others came. It was the four guys from the beginning of the week and a girl.

"Guys this is joey, she's letting us stay here tonight while we have a few drinks. We've got boundaries though. So we all have to respect joeys home and listen to her." Lauren said.

"Ok." They all shrugged and came in. I set them in one of the games room.

"This is amazing." The other girl looked around the room. It has a bar, pool table and bowling alley with arcade games.

"Thanks." I mumbled.

"Joey, let me introduce you to everyone. This is Harriette Carmichael, Grayson Webb, miles and Hendrix Montgomery and my cousin Abbott stone." Lauren pointed to everyone.

Harriette had pink dyed hair with dull green eyes. Miles and Hendrix both had sandy blonde hair with blue eyes. Lastly, Abbott had dark brown hair with red streaks and blue eyes.

"How the hell did you afford all this?" Hendrix looked at me with shock.

"My job is something I don't really like to get into. Not when it's personal to me anyway." I looked down to the floor.

"Well then, let's party!" Harriette yelled making every one, but me and Abbott, cheer.

At around 8pm, I got a phone call. "I've got to take this." I stood up and left the room.

"Hello?" I answered.

"Ah, Miss Smith. I need another job for you to do. But I know your a very busy girl but I need you."

"How much?" I asked.

"For this one its double. $4 billion and it'll be worth it."

"Yeah. Like usual, when and where and you know I'll be there." I said then hung up.

'Venice beach. Outside Antonio's club 9:30pm.' The message came through.

I shut off my phone then went back into the games room. Lauren, Harriette, Grayson, miles and Hendrix were all playing pool while Abbott sat by the bar.

"Hey guys, I have to go out for a couple hours. I'll be back around midnight so you can do whatever. Just ask Lauren the boundaries and make sure to stick to it." I announced.

"Where are you going?" Hendrix frowned at me.

"Just to meet some family. They like to keep me around a lot that's why I'll be back late. I have to go get ready but help yourselves to anything." I told them then went up to my room.

I put on my usual black jeans and T-shirt with my long black coat and combat boots. I put my hair up in a high pony tail with my bandana in my pocket ready to put over my face.

I went into my weapons room and put an AK47 rifle in a bag. Before anyone could stop me, I shouted bye and left the house.

Chapter 4. Old 'friend'

Joey POV

It's now Monday and I'm at school. Lauren refused to take the care so I had to pick her up.

"Why can't you just take the car? It's a gift so you can get to places without relying on others." I whined.

"Because it's to much." She replied.

"Then will you accept money to get yourself one? Even if you get a cheap one then give the rest of the money to your family."

"I can't joey."

"What if I told you that I have to much? That it will help me more than you if you take a car or money." I asked.

"That's because it won't. It'll be helping my family more than anything." Lauren sighed.

"What's going on with your family?" I questioned.

"My mom and dad aren't really, how can I put it? They don't like to work. They rely on my aunt and uncle for money. Abbott's parents.

But last year they cut them off since they kept on asking for so much."
Lauren explained.

I could hear the sadness in her voice as she looked out the window,
avoiding my eyes.

"What do they spend the money on?" I pressed on.

"Gambling, alcohol, drugs. As soon as my aunt and uncle found
out, they said no to more money. That they needed to get real jobs so
they can support me and my little brother."

"Lauren stone, will you please accept my offer of a car and $2
million dollars. I need to get rid of it and you really need it. It'll be
enough for you to do whatever you want with it." I begged.

"Joey I can't. They'll just waste it all on drugs their gambling debts
and drinks." A few tears fell from her eyes.

"Then take it all, keep it a secret to help you and your brother.
Please, it'll make me feel better knowing my best friend is ok." I
parked the car then looked at her.

"Ok. I don't know how to thank you joey. Thank you so much."
Lauren cried.

"Don't cry. I wanted to. Now wipe your eyes and walk into that
school like you own the damn place." I smiled at her.

"Thank you."

"Don't mention it. I'm glad I can help."

We both walked into the school, only to be greeted by Harriette ,
Grayson, Hendrix, miles and Abbott.

"Are you ok? Why have you been crying?" Abbott went over to
Lauren.

"I have but they were happy tears. Joey kindly gave me money so I can support me and Kenny." She told him.

"Ok. Get to class then, I'll see you later." Abbott hugged her then everyone walked off.

As I went to leave, I was stopped. "How much did you give her? I can pay you back." Abbott said.

"Listen, Lauren is my only friend here. I don't have many of those, and the ones I do have live elsewhere. I have enough to give it to Lauren and to keep me stable, don't pay me back, because I will only give it back. She told me about her and her little brother, just let me do this. It'll be a win win for both of us." I told him.

"How?" He asked.

"Because the amount of money I'm giving Lauren, is what I make every night. Good bye Abbott, don't make Lauren feel bad about it." I smiled at him then left to go to class.

Abbott PoV

I watched her as she walked away. The way she carried herself was very similar to how I do it. She's very different.

I just need to figure out how she can afford a house like that. Maybe she's in the gang life like me.

Not a chance. With a big house like that, she would face members around, I can't place it, but that one, she is something else.

Joey POV

"So I was thinking maybe we can go to your house tonight. Skip school tomorrow and just have some fun." Lauren suggested.

"I'm down. Who'll be there?" I asked.

"Same as Friday night. Is that ok?"

"Of course. I have to go out again tonight but I'll be done before 11." I told her.

"Definitely. The others will meet us there." Lauren laughed nervously.

"I'm guessing you already knew my answer?"

"Yeah. I would have texted them if you said otherwise. But they should be there now."

We got into my car and I drove back to my house.

When we got there, everyone was waiting outside my front door.

"There she is." Harriette cheered.

"Did you all bring what I told you to?" Lauren smiled at them all.

"What's that?" I asked.

"Swim suits. I noticed you had a pool and I was wondering if we could go in it."

"Of course. As long as you all keep out of the third floor, I don't care where you go." I replied with a shrug.

"Let's party!" Grayson and Harriette both yelled.

I opened the door and something felt off.

"Someone's in here." I stated.

"What do you mean?" Miles asked.

"I mean someone is in my house. I'm not sure who though." I replied.

We all dropped our bags and I put my hand over my hand gun just in case I needed it.

I walked around slowly and carefully so I wouldn't be heard.

We got to the games room and I saw someone sat at the bar with their backs to me. They had a long black coat on and black hair. I knew who it was.

There was a tennis ball close by so I picked it up and threw it at the persons back.

"You scared the shit out of me you damn prick." I scolded him.

"Thought I might surprise my little as-," he began but I cut him off.

"Nope. Not that name here. I have my friends here." I told him. He turned around and gave me a huge smile.

"Finally got into school then? That's a surprise." He faked being shocked.

"Shut up. Why are you here anyway?" I hugged him.

"We've got a job to do. Except we have to go to Vegas."

"You know I work alone. Tell him I'm staying here and if he wants it so bad, he can come get my himself."

"You know your the best. Come on Callie. We can make a road trip of it." He whined.

"No! That is my final answer." I glared at him.

"Fine." He crossed his arms over like a child.

"Ah hem. Who's this?" Grayson asked.

"Oh sorry. This is my friend Elliot. Elliot this is Lauren, Harriette, Grayson, miles, Hendrix and Abbott." I introduced them.

"You know the guys are in a gang right?" Elliot whispered to me.

"Yes, they just don't know about me." I whispered back.

"Well let's get this party started." Lauren yelled. This is going to be one long night.

Chapter 5. Didn't expect that.

J oey POV

We were all sat in my pool. Elliot had become friendly with Lauren and Harriette was with Grayson.

"Do you have anyone special in your life joey?" Elliot asked me.

"You know I don't. I'm to busy for boys and I don't need one nor want one." I told him.

"Come on. Remember Will from Chicago? He still asks about you."

"Well I don't. He needs to move on and it was only a petty crush because I was better than all of you boys."

"You know it baby. How's Miguel anyway?" Elliot changed the subject.

"Good. I'm going to see him, Gloria and the kids later after I'm done with my job." I replied.

"Oh is that the family you went to see Friday night? The one that talks a lot." Harriette asked.

"Yeah. They're Columbian. They were the ones who took me in when I was dumped here." I responded.

"So what's your life story joey?" Grayson joined in.

"Not much. Parents died when I was three. I was adopted then my life changed when I was four. At thirteen was dumped here in LA and Miguel and his wife took me in. I stayed with them for a couple months then got myself a small apartment. Then when I was fifteen, I brought this place. That's all really." I shrugged.

"How did you get all the money?" Hendrix pressed on.

"That's a story for another time. I've got to go meet Miguel. I'll be back around 11. Are you coming dimwit?" I turned to Elliot.

"Hells yeah. I haven't seen that pedazo de hombre in a long time." Elliot laughed.

"He does look good for his age doesn't he." I chuckled.

"What did you just say?" Miles furrowed his eyebrows.

"I called him a hunk of a man. He's pretty sexy for a man and he's 43 so he's not bad looking for his age." Elliot shrugged and got out of the pool.

"Can we come? We would love to meet Miguel." Lauren smiled.

"He's fluent Spanish and doesn't like people he doesn't know." Elliot lied.

"And no offence Lauren, you talk a lot so it would be to much for them to translate. Let's just hang here and go another time." Harriette said.

"Yeah your right." Lauren pouted.

"Come on then. Let's go." Elliot put his hand out for me. I grabbed it and he pulled me up so my feet was stable on the ground.

"How fucking strong are you?" Hendrix gasped at Elliot.

"Long story. Let's go." He replied. We both went inside and up to our rooms.

Yes. Elliot has a room here since he visits me a lot and stays long periods of time.

I changed into my usual black outfit and coat. When I opened my door, Elliot smirked at me.

"I love this room." He got excited when we entered my weapons room.

I put in two snipers in a bag then we both left.

"Bye guys. We'll see you later." I stood by the door.

"Why are you in all black? And them coats." Hendrix laughed.

"It's a tradition. Don't ask, bye." I shouted.

"What's in the bag?" Abbott called out.

"As dead body." I said bluntly. Everyone's faces dropped. "I'm joking. Presents for the kids. They're five and seven years old."

"Bye guys." Lauren waved them we left.

"They really like to ask questions don't they." Elliot said when we got into my car.

"Yeah but they're good people. I'm starting to have doubts about being friends with them." I sighed and started driving.

"I'm sure you will be able to keep them safe. It'll be all good. So what are we going tonight?"

"There is a Gang stand off. They are going a trade and the guy who called me wants me to be there so if shit hits the fan, we can take down the other group." I told him.

"Perfect. Are we going halves on the pay?"

"Of course. What friend would I be if I didn't. It's group work." I nudged him a little.

We got to the place and went up on top of a building. My phone started ringing but I already knew who it was.

"Hello?"

"Are you here?"

"Yep. I have a friend as well so if it all goes wrong you have two sharp shooters."

"How do i know you're really here?"

I set up my gun and shot near his foot making the gang leader jump back. He looked up in my direction and I waved little.

"That's me sunshine. I always keep my end of the deal. Now get this over with, I have guests back at my home." I said then hung up.

The rival gang came and started doing the deal. Of course, shit hit the fan and the rival pulled his gun out. Before he could shoot, I pulled my trigger and he went down.

Both me and Elliot shot most of the rival gang and others got away.

When it was clear, we both went down with our bandanas over our faces to get the money.

"Thank you for that. Very well done miss smith. This is for you. The $3 million I offered. And that's for your friend, he's got two since it was all I had on me." The gang leader gave me two envelopes.

"Happy to help anytime." I said then left.

"Here, you got two million. He said it was all he had on top of mine. But I can still half it with you." I handed Elliot his money.

"Nope. Two million is good for me. Now let's get back to party." Elliot cheered. We got back into my car and went back to my house.

When we got there, we went out to the pool to make sure everyone was ok.

That's when I saw him. The one man who made my life hell.

Chapter 6. Pablo

Joey POV

When we got there, we went out to the pool to make sure everyone was ok.

That's when I saw him. The one man who made my life hell.

~~~~~~~~~~~~~~~~~~~~~~~~~~~

"What the fuck are you doing here?" I glared at him. Abbott, Lauren, Miles, Grayson, Harriette and Hendrix were all looking at him with strange looks.

"I've come to see my best worker. I've missed you a lot joey." He smirked at me.

"You have no right to come here." I gritted out.

"Oh but I do. Come now joey, shall we discuss business. I'm sure Elliot has told you all about Vegas."

"You need to leave now, Pablo. I work on my own, ever since you put me on the streets. Now get out of my house."

"Don't be like that mi amor. You know I loved you like you was my own blood. Come give me a hug." Pablo put his arms out.

"No! I'm going to get changed, and you need to be gone by the time I get back or I'll get you out myself." I glared at him then left with Elliot hot on my trail.

"Did you know he was coming?" I turned to Elliot on the stairs. My eyes were hard and the only emotion showing was hurt.

"Yes. I was hoping you would say yes to the trip so we could get the job over with and Pablo wouldn't have come here." He looked down.

"Give everyone a room and tell them I'll see them tomorrow. Keep them from my floor and make sure Pablo is gone." I said then left him.

I changed into shorts and a tank top and flopped on my bed. Why did he have to show up?

Abbott's POV

When joey left, we all stayed in the pool. There had to be something wrong with her and Elliot.

"They're weird. Maybe they had a thing." Harriette shrugged leaning into Grayson.

"Now I feel bad." Lauren pouted.

"Why?" Hendrix furrowed his eyebrows.

"Me and Elliot were cozying up to each other. If they were a thing then she still might have feelings. I feel like a horrible friend." Lauren sighed.

"I'm sure she's over it. Don't beat yourself up." Miles smiled softly at her.

"They weren't together." I rolled my eyes.

"What?" They all blurted out.

"They were never a thing. If anything, they are like brother and sister. Don't worry about it Lauren, I think he likes you anyway." I shrugged.

"Thanks cuz. Always know how to make me feel better." Lauren smiled a little.

After a while a man came from the house.

"Excuse me? Who are you?" Harriette frowned.

"Ah, you must be joeys friends. I'm like a father to her. I've just come to see my little... girl." The man said.

"Ok. Well she's seeing some family at the moment. I guess you could stay if you are close to Joey." Lauren shrugged.

"Perfecto. Gracias niña." He said.

"Your Spanish? Does that mean you know Miguel?" Miles asked him.

"Who? No I don't know him." He replied. "I'm guessing that's who she's gone to see."

"Yeah. Where else would she be?" Lauren scoffed.

"So she hasn't told you her secret then?" The man smiled darkly.

"No what secret?" Harriette furrowed her eyebrows.

"What the fuck are you doing here?" I heard a pissed off joey behind us. We all looked at her and the man smirked.

"I've come to see my best worker. I've missed you a lot joey."

"You have no right to come here." Joey glared at him. Elliot had a similar look towards the man.

Oh but I do. Come now joey, shall we discuss business. I'm sure Elliot has told you about Vegas." The man raised one eyebrow.

"You need to leave now Pablo. I work on my own, ever since you put me on the streets. Now get out of my house." Joey said obviously not playing any games.

"Don't be like that mi amor. You know I loved you like you was my own blood. Come give me a hug." The man smirked and put his arms out.

"No! I'm going to get changed and you need to be gone by the time I get back or I'll get you out myself." She glared at him then left.

Elliot followed joey but came back minutes later. "I'll show you all to different rooms. Joey just needs some time to process this all."

"We understand. Is she ok?" Laurens eyes were soft.

"Yeah. She's stronger than you think. She'll be fine tomorrow morning." He shrugged. "Pablo, you need to leave now. Joey will contact you when she's ready. Goodbye."

"Fine. But I will see you both in Vegas." Pablo had a hard stare then left. We all stayed silent as we all followed Elliot into the house.

When we got to the second floor, and Elliot all gave us our own rooms. Grayson and Harriette both went in one room, Lauren and Elliot in another. Miles and Hendrix chose to share as they are brothers.

"You can go in that one. Unless you want to share with someone." Elliot pointed to the end room.

"No it's all good. I'm going to go get a drink then I'll go to bed. Thanks." I replied then went to the stairs.

Instead of going to get a drink, I went up to the third floor to see it exactly the same as the second.

I checked all the rooms and came across one that I took an interest to. It was full of guns. Hand guns, rifles, snipers. Bullets were stashed on the walls with a couple hand guns next to the ammo.

"What are you doing in here?" A voice said behind me.

Chapter 7. Secrets spilled

A bbott's POV

"What are you doing in here?" A voice said behind me.

I turned around to see joey leaned against the door. She looked angry but also like she didn't care.

"I can leave." I said bluntly.

"Don't bother. Why are you in here? I'm sure Lauren told you all that this floor is off limits."

"Yes she did. I was just coming to see if you were ok." Just like joey, I didn't have any emotion in my eyes and my facial expression was neutral.

"And you just so happened to find my gun room? Sounds to me like you were snooping around." Joey crosses her arms over her chest.

"Like I said, I can leave." I glared at her.

"Sure. But I must warn you." She took a step closer to me. "If you tell anyone about this, I will not hesitate to kill you. I have a name and an alibi."

"What happened to you?" I asked genuinely curious about this small, petite girl with this many weapons.

"I could use a drink." She changed the subject.

"Joey." I grabbed her wrist. "What happened to you?"

"Come on. Let's go talk downstairs." Joey looked down and lead me out of the room, shutting the door behind us.

We got downstairs and went into a small room. There was a bar with a lot of spirits and soft drinks.

Joey poured us both a bourbon and sat down next to me on a stall.

"Why do you want to know what happened to me? I could just be some deranged psychopath with weapons in her house." Joey broke the silence.

"Because I know something is off. You are far from a psychopath. Maybe telling someone will do you some good." I shrugged and took a sip of my drink.

"My parents died when I was three. I lived in Chicago but after their death I was put in an orphanage. A couple adopted me only to get money. When I was four they sold me off to get more of that money." She sighed.

"All of my childhood was made up of Pablo beating me, training me to be the greatest there is. That is how I know Elliot, we were partners. Then when I was thirteen, Pablo put me on the streets of great Los Angeles." Joey closed her eyes.

"Miguel took me in with his wife Gloria and their 2 year old. Gloria was pregnant with another son but wanted a daughter so they took me in. But of course, Pablo didn't let me go so easily. He kicked me out with a phone and the only clothes on my back." She opened her eyes again.

"Every time that phone rang I was making a name for myself. People used me and paid me a lot of money. Eventually I got myself a small apartment. With all the jobs I had to do, there wasn't anytime for school or to learn anything. The only thing I ever knew was to keep my emotions down and not let anyone in." Her eyes glossed over.

"So at age thirteen I knew nothing. Then you know the good old times when a young girl blooms. I had to ask Gloria if it was all natural. She told me all I needed to know. Changes my body will make, feelings, hormones. But of course, with all my fucked up life, I left once I knew everything. I still see them but not as much as I did."

"What did Pablo do to you?" I asked.

"I was trained all my life to become an assassin. I've killed many men. Gangs, mafias. Ever heard of the name Joey smith?" She questioned me.

"Yeah. Everyone has."

"Have you ever wanted to know what she looks like?"

"Hasn't everyone. Why are you asking me this?" I furrowed my eyebrows.

"Because you're looking at her right now." Joey sipped her drink.

"How do I know your not lying?"

"That room upstairs for one. When I left earlier, I went to help out a gang leader. This house. How else do you think I get the money to pay for it?" She laughed.

"What else did he do to you and Elliot?"

"Beat us. We were not allowed to cry, call out for help. Over time I became the best shooter in the whole place. As I was the only girl, boys wanted me other then Elliot. They got their hormones and wanted more but as I was the best, I was able to defend myself and with the help of Elliot. Joey and Elliot isn't our real names." Joey looked down.

"What are they?" I pressed on.

"Callie. I'm Callie Rose. Elliot is Humphrey Addams. We were given names so people would fear us."

"Why don't you stop?"

"I can't. The only way out is death. I can't change my identity because Pablo will always find out and come to get me. I'm in this for life." Joey said.

"I'm sorry."

"No your not." She took a sip of bourbon. "You only said it because I was beat and changed. It doesn't matter anyway. I like who I am and it won't change."

"I'm in a gang. Me, Miles, Hendrix and Grayson. My dad is Craig stone. Lauren doesn't know though. That's how my parents were able to help her, but we had to cut them off. I assume she told you since you gave her money." I sighed.

"Yeah. I felt bad so I gave her money and a car." Joey laughed a little.

"How many cars do you have?"

"I'll show you around." Joey smirked then stood up.

Damn, things I could do to this girl. She shouldn't be smirking around me.

Stop it. You've only met her a week ago. Just stop.

After that, Joey showed me her whole house. From the garage to all her games rooms, living room, kitchen, second floor and the third.

She said that the whole of the third floor was hers and out of bounds to everyone, except her and Elliot.

"Goodnight Abbott." Joey smiled a little.

"Goodnight Joey. Or Callie. I don't know what to call you." I chuckled nervously.

"Joey will be fine." She giggled then walked away. She is one crazy girl.

Chapter 8. Moving in

Joey POV

"What are you doing later?" Lauren and Harriette smile widely at me, with they boys behind her.

"Not much. I have a job to do with Elliot and that's it." I replied. When I finished my sentence, I heard Abbott cough.

I smirked knowing that he knows where I'm going.

"Well, we want to have a small party. It won't be huge and I'll make sure no one goes on your secret floor." Lauren begged.

"You know I'm always down for a party but i can't tonight. Tomorrow definitely, I'm not working but I can't tonight." I told her.

"Deal." She giggled. Before I could say anything, I was cut off by my phone ringing.

"I have to take this." I excused myself and walked away.

"Hello?" I answered.

"Hola joey. Glad you still have the same number." Pablos voice came through the phone.

"What the fuck do you want pablo? I'm in school I don't have time to be dealing with your bullshit." I made my voice angry.

"Don't be like that joey. I have a job. I'm paying you $10 million to get it done."

"Why can't you do it yourself?"

"Because no one is as good as you. So what do to say?" I could hear the smirk in his voice.

"Fine. When and where?"

"Tomorrow at Griffith park, be there by 11pm. I need Gregory Daniels killed. Don't worry mi amor, I will have all the money there." With that he hung up.

"Are you going?" A deep voice said behind me.

"I have no choice. I'll take Elliot with me so he can't try anything."

"I can go with you. That way Lauren can still have her party and Elliot can make sure no one goes in your room."

"Are you sure you can handle me killing someone? Elliot can't." I turned around.

"I've seen my dad do it. I think I'll be fine."

"Fine. You can have half the pay for going with me." I told him.

"I don't need money."

"Well I need to get rid of some of it. Just take it Abbott. Then you can give it away or get whatever you want with it." I shrugged.

"Fine. What do I need to do while we're there?" Abbott asked.

"Not much. I'll do it all. Just remember to stay low and not get in my way." I told him then walked off.

The day went by pretty quickly, everyone went back to my place so they could enjoy the pool in the heat.

While we were there, Abbott swam over to me.

"What time are you leaving tonight?" He asked.

"9. It four now so I'll be getting ready at 8. Why?"

"Just wondering. So, what was your first kill like?"

"Not much. I was thirteen, killed a man called Alex shaw. Got $3 million for it. Gave most of it to Miguel and Gloria so they could open their own liquor store. Keep them on their feet with their son Juan and their other son Diego." I told him.

"How did you feel?" Abbott looked at me.

"Nothing. That's how Pablo trained me. You don't feel anything, you just get the job done, get the money and leave."

"Callie, what time are we leaving tonight?" Elliot called over to me.

"At 9. But your staying here. I'm going to do it on my own. I'll be staying out after as well so I won't be home til late." I told him.

"Ok. I need to talk to you anyway." He swam over.

"I need to move in. Pablo kicked me out of the main house." Elliot talked lowly because of Abbott.

"You can talk normally El, Abbott knows." I closed my eyes and leaned my head back.

"Ok. Well please can I move in? I'll help pay for everything as well." Elliot begged me.

"Yeah. You have your own room. The only thing you need to pay for is food. Leave the rest to me."

"Thank god. I don't get as many jobs as you so that's a relief."

"It's ok. Just tell me if you bring girls home, that way i can get earplugs to drown out the noise." I rolled my eyes.

"Deal. Bye." Elliot smiled then went back over to Lauren.

"Do you want company tonight?" Abbott looked at me.

"Sure. After we have to make a detour so be prepared to be smothered by Spanish people and their kids." I smirked.

"No problem. I'll be able to learn tonight then I'll be a pro tomorrow."

"Sure. Whatever helps you pretty boy. But I'm picking your outfit. That way you won't be seen and I won't get caught."

"I'm pretty sure the police shit themselves when they hear your name." Abbott laughed.

"Maybe." I chuckled.

"I have a question?" Hendrix came over with the others.

"What may that be?" I looked at them all.

"Why does Elliot call you Callie?" Miles furrowed his eyebrows.

"Because that's my name. I have two names, one that everyone calls me, Joey. And Callie is something only Elliot can call me. So don't be getting any ideas." I replied.

"Right. So why do you have people call you joey when it's not your actual name?" Grayson said.

"Because that's her middle name. Elliot only calls her Callie to piss her off. She prefers to be called joey." Abbott lied.

"How did you know that?" Lauren looked between me and Abbott.

"Because we are the best of friends aren't we joey?" He put one arm around my shoulders.

"Sure. That's totally why." I rolled my eyes.

"Is there something going on with you two? Like more than friends?" Harriette asked.

"Yep. Joey here has a little crush on me. Isn't that right." Abbott smirked.

"Yes Abbott. I am so in love with you that I want you to kiss me and tell me you love me so much." I said sarcastically.

"Joey your a damn virgin. You don't know how to kiss a boy." Elliot laughed.

"I may be a virgin but I know how to kiss a guy. You on the other hand, can't kiss a girl. One you are also a virgin and second, I was the only girl there and I always turned you down."

"Way to rat me out joey. Thanks so much." Elliot rolled his eyes.

"Abbott will take your kissing virginity joey." Grayson smirked.

"Yes. Kiss her Abbott." Lauren squealed.

"Go on Abbott. You've been moaning that you haven't gotten any." Miles chuckled.

"No can do guys. Joey is the one with the crush on me." Abbott winked at me.

"Of course. Kiss me please Abbott, my oh so sexy crush." I said sarcastically again.

He leaned in and connected our lips. We both moved our lips together, Abbott squeezed my thigh causing me to gasp and he stuck his tongue in my mouth.

My hands went around his neck while he went to my waist. In that moment it was only me and Abbott.

I could feel the butterflies in my stomach and my heart fluttering at his touch. His hands on my bare skin made me want more.

When we pulled away, we were breathing heavily just looking into each other's eyes.

"That was hot." Harriette blurted out.

Just then, they all started cheering and clapping.

"I have to get ready." I stated.

"I'll come with you." Abbott said and followed me out of the pool.

Chapter 9. The kiss

Joey POV

I quickly got out of the pool so I could get away from everyone. I'm sure my cheeks were bright red and my face resembled a tomato.

When I got inside, the door closed behind me. My wrist was grabbed and I was turned around, bumping into a hard chest.

Abbott looked down at me, our lips were close and we just looked into each other's eyes. He lifted up his hand and started playing with a strand of my hair and I closed my eyes.

"Why did you do that?" I whispered.

"You have no idea how long I've wanted to do that. Trust me, it's been a long damn time." Abbott told me.

I couldn't say anything else. All I could do was look at this sexy man in front of me. We didn't say anything, we just stood there and looked at each other.

All of a sudden, Abbott closed the gap and put his lips on mine. It wasn't rough and fast like the one in the pool, it was slow and steady.

We pulled away when we needed air, but kept our foreheads together. I could feel my lips swollen and Abbott's looked how mine felt.

"For a first time kisser you're really good." He chuckled.

"Shut up." I smiled a little and pushed his shoulder. "Come on. We don't have long until we have to leave."

I grabbed his hand and pulled him up to my room.

"Here. Put these on." I handed him black jeans, T-shirt, coat and boots.

"And you expect me to get changed in front of you?" Abbott raised one eyebrow.

"No. Go shower in my en-suite then you can change in there. I don't want you smelling like chlorine when you meet Miguel and his wife." I told him.

"Right. And he knows about you taking me?"

"Not exactly. Now go change before I lose my money and someone doesn't die." I ordered and pushed him into the bathroom.

I quickly got my clothes then went into Elliot's room to shower and change. After I washed my hair and body, I dried myself and on my usual black outfit.

Once I left the room, I headed up to my floor, bumping into Abbott.

"Sorry." I mumbled.

"No problem." He replied. I carried on walking as he followed behind me.

I unlocked the door and went into the weapons room. "I will never be able to get used to this." Abbott looked around.

"I've had this room for four years. It's nothing compared to my other room." I laughed.

I got one sniper and put it in my bag. "Why are you only talking one?" Abbott asked.

"Because I don't need you shooting any of the wrong people. I need the money to keep me going." I told him.

"You know I'm in a gang right?" He chuckled.

"Yeah. I remember you telling me the night I told you about myself."

"Heard of the name Abbott stone?"

"Yeah. No one knows what he looks like. He's like me but I work alone." I shrugged.

"Now you know what he looks like. I know how to use a sniper and I know who to kill if needs be." Abbott said.

"Damn. I always thought Abbott stone would be a old grumpy bastard with to much time on his hands. Not some hot teenager." I froze when I realised what I had said.

"You think I'm hot?" He bit his bottom lip and smirked.

"Yeah. Remember my oh so deep crush on you?" I asked with sarcasm lacing my voice. Then busied myself by putting a second sniper in my bag.

"I don't think I do." Abbott walked over to me, putting his hands on my hips. "Care to remind me?"

"Oh sure. I don't mind that at all." I rolled my eyes. Once again, sarcasm in my voice.

"Come on. We don't want to be late do we?" He smirked then picked up the bag.

We both went back to the others, saying a quick goodbye and left in my car.

When we got to the destination, I took Abbott to a hiding spot then set up both guns. Eventually, both gangs showed up and I got my target.

"What are we waiting for?" Abbott whispered to me.

"Not much. I just need the right time to shoot." I replied.

"What if there was a distraction and you couldn't kill your target?" He smirked and raised one eyebrow.

"I can still kill them. Pablo trained me to keep focus no matter what distraction was around."

"So what if I did this?" Abbott got up and went behind me. I felt his hard chest against my back.

His warm breath fanned on my neck as his lips trailed down. Just then, he started laying soft kisses on my neck.

I felt one of his hands travel down my side, to my waist then to the inside of my thigh. I closed my eyes for a second then opened them to keep focused.

His lips danced around my neck as his hand went higher up my thigh. Abbott started biting and sucking on my skin, surely leaving hickeys.

As I went to close my eyes again, I saw my target go to pull out his gun. Before he could pull the trigger, my bullet entered his head. From where I was, I could hear the third of his body hitting the ground.

"You don't know how much that turned me on." Abbott whispered in my ear huskily. I could feel myself getting turned on by his hand close to my lower region and his lips sucking on my neck.

"Told you I could still kill someone." I breathed out. "We have to go. I need to get my money."

"I want to take you right here right now." Abbott said then pulled me so my back went to the floor. When I was laying down, he spread my legs open with his knees and went between them.

Abbott put his hands by my head and leaned down, kissing me hungrily. I could feel his hard member against my now aching core.

A moan escaped lips into his mouth. He kissed me with so much force and need. I didn't waste a moment to kiss back with the same amount of need.

"Ah hem." A person cleared their throat making Abbott pull away from me. We both looked up to see the gang leader that called me.

"Miss smith I assume." He looked down at me.

"Shit." I muttered.

"Don't worry. I'll keep your face a secret, but I must say your are a beautiful one." The man smirked. "Here's your money. Thank you for your help."

With that, he threw me an envelope and walked away. I put the money in my coat pocket and pushed Abbott off me.

"We've got to go to Miguel's now." I mumbled and stood up.

"What am I supposed to do with this?" Abbott gestured to his very prominent erection.

"You can sit in the back of my car and sort yourself out." I shrugged.

"You expect me to jerk off so in the back of your car so I can get rid of it?"

"Yes now hurry up." I ordered. I packed up both guns then went back my car.

Chapter 10. Meeting Miguel

Abbott POV

Me and joey made our way over to her blue Lamborghini. She kept on making jokes and laughing about me trying to walk with my very hard shaft.

"Stop laughing." I whined. "You wouldn't like it if you were like this."

"Trust me, I know what it's like to be like... that." Joey laughed.

"I don't see you with a boner. Now stop laughing." I glared at her.

"Seriously? Do you want to put your hands down my jeans and feel me?"

"Is that a rhetorical question?" I asked.

"Shut up. Do you know how frustrated I am right now?" She whined while putting the bag in the trunk.

"Feelings mutual. So what are we doing with your Spanish family?" I asked once we both got in the car.

"Not much. The kids will want to play but other than that, we should be good." Joey shrugged then started driving.

"Isn't it late for kids their age to be up? Aren't they what? Seven and five?"

"Yeah but they are Latino. They are crazy." She laughed.

"Where did you learn Spanish?"

"Pablo. I was only four when he brought me off the couple that adopted me. Therefore, being the youngest, I was taught the language. I'm originally from Chicago." Joey explained.

"Soy fluido en el idioma. Así es como me Hanson los niños." Joey said.

"That was hot." I smirked. "What does it mean?"

"I said, I am fluent in the language. That is how the kids speak to me."

"Well please don't speak Spanish. It's not helping with my problem." I groaned.

"Whatever. You know they don't speak much English so I will have to do it. Just make sure you keep them hormones down." Joey chuckled and pulled up to a liquor store.

"A liquor store?" I raised a questioning brow.

"Yep." She nodded popping the p. "For my first kill, I gave Gloria and Miguel most of the money so they could get this place."

We both got out of the car, thank god my hard on went down otherwise that would leave a great first impression. Note the sarcasm.

"Mi pequeño asesina." A short man cheered.

"Miguel, do you want to wake the niños?" A woman scolded the man.

"Hola Gloria. Como estas?" Joey smiled widely.

"Joey. Soy bueno." The woman yelled.

Just then, two small boys walked in from the back, running their eyes.

"Papa? Ma-," the oldest one started but stopped when he saw joey. "JOEY!"

Both kids ran up to her, wrapping their arms around her legs.

"Hey guys. Shouldn't you be asleep?" Joey smiled down at them.

"No. Mama said we can wait up to see you. We wanted you to tuck us into bed." The oldest gave her a huge toothy grin.

"Is that so? I thought tonight you would sleep and Joey would see you tomorrow after school. She hasn't got as much time on her hands as she used to." The man glared at the woman a little.

"Cállate." The woman flipped him off.

"Ok. Guys this is my friend Abbott. He goes to school with me." Joey pointed to me. "Abbott this is Miguel, his amazing wife Gloria and their two sons, Juan and Diego."

"Nice to meet you Abbott." The man smiled at me.

"You to." I gave him a tight lipped smile.

"Are you her novio?" The youngest, Diego tapped my leg.

"Uh. I don't speak Spanish." I laughed nervously.

"No Diego. Just my amigo." Joey told him.

"Where's Elliot tonight? Isn't he usually with you?" Miguel asked joey.

"He's with one of my other friends from school. She's really nice and Abbott's cousin, that's partly how I know him."

"Well we should meet your other amigos soon." Gloria clapped her hands.

"Yeah sure. They just don't know what I am so when they come just keep it on the down low." Joey told them.

"Of course. We wouldn't want certain people to know your secret." Miguel looked at me for a second.

"He knows so it's ok. Actually, I have my stuff in the car, is it ok if I leave it here tonight? I just want to go straight home and sleep." Joey looked at them tiredly.

"Of course you can. No hay problema querida." Gloria smiled softly.

"Gracias." Joey said then went outside with Diego on her leg.

"So." Miguel looked at me. "What are your intentions with joey?"

"I'm just a friend. That's it." I told him.

"Ok. Make sure she stays away from boys. I know what they are like nowadays."

"Miguel." His wife shot him a glare. "Joey can go out with boys if she wants to."

"Who can go out with boys?" Joey came back in. She had Diego in one arm and the bag in the other.

"Miguel was telling Abbott that he should keep boys away from you. You're old enough to look after yourself so you can have a boyfriend if you want." Gloria shrugged.

"Thanks for the concern. But I don't want a boyfriend nor need one. I'm good on my own." Joey laughed.

"Ok. Well it's late so kids, get to bed. Joey will come by again soon so you will have more time with her." Miguel said.

"Yes. I don't have work on the weekend so you can come to my house and play in the pool, have a sleepover and stuff our faces with junk food and watch movies until you pass out." Joey said excitedly.

"Yes!" Both kids screamed.

"Gracias Joey. You know they love you like an older hermana." Gloria smiled at her.

"Night guys. I'll pick you up Friday so be ready." Joey put Diego on the floor.

"Buenos noches Joey. Nice to meet you Abbott." Both kids waved at me then left with their mother.

"Have a good night both of you. Remember, no boys." Miguel hugged Joey.

"Your the only man in my life Miguel, I don't need anyone else." She joked.

"That's how it should stay. Nice to meet you Abbott, I'll see you Friday when you pick up the boys." Miguel hugged joey then we left.

When we got back to joeys house, everyone was in bed so we went our separate ways and went to our own rooms.

Chapter 11. Sleepover

- -

Joey POV

"You guys ready?" I smiled down at Juan and Diego.

"Yeah." They both had huge smiled on their faces.

"Here you go." Gloria handed me the bag of guns I had left there. "Take care of my boys and don't let them stay up past 11."

"You know me, no one will hurt them. I have my friends there tonight as well so it'll be fine. All the boys are in a gang and Elliot is living with me now so all will be good." I reassured her.

"Is Abbott there?" Juan asked me.

"He's always there. It's like they live with me." I joked.

"Ok let's go." Diego pulled my hand.

"Have fun and stay safe. Bye kids." Miguel called after us.

"Bye dad." We all called back. I put the bags in the trunk then helped Juan and Diego I'm the car with their seatbelts.

It was a short car ride with a lot of music and loud singing from all of us. When we got in, I took out all the bags and headed in.

As soon as the door opened, Juan and Diego ran in screaming. Their usual reaction when they come here.

"Abbott." The boys yelled then ran up to him.

"Hey kiddos. Are you excited for tonight?" Abbott picked both of them up.

"Yep." Diego nodded while popping the p.

"Am I not your favourite anymore? Me siento herido." Elliot put one hand on his chest.

"Hold Elliot. You're still my favourite." Juan jumped down and ran to him.

"Guys this is Juan and Diego. Miguel's boys, they will be staying with me for the night so no drinking." I warned them.

"Eye eye captain." Lauren and Harriette saluted me.

"God." I laughed. "Elliot can you put this in my room. Or are you good to look after the boys for a few?"

"I can watch them. I don't really know how to do it like you so I can't." He shrugged.

"I want to go with you." Juan clung on to my leg.

"Come on then. Diego are you staying with Elliot?" I turned to him.

"No. Me quedo con Abbott." Diego said.

"Fine. I'll be down in a few minutes then we can go in the pool since the sun is still high." I smiled then left with Juan.

I got up to my weapons room and started putting both snipers away.

Juan let go of my leg and started wondering around. While I had my back to him, I couldn't see what he was doing.

"Put it down Juan. You don't want to hurt yourself." I said while keeping my eyes on the sniper in my hands.

"How did you know?" He asked sounding shocked.

"Do you not know what my job is?" I turned to him.

"Si. Papa tells me stories from when you was younger. Like bedtime stories." Juan said.

"You can't tell any of my friends downstairs, ok? Only Abbott and Elliot know. I'm not ready to tell Lauren, Harriette and the other boys."

"Cruza mi corazón." Juan put his hand over his heart.

"Gracias. Now let's get this done and get in the pool." I smiled. I quickly put both snipers away then went back downstairs giving Juan a piggy back ride.

When we got to the living room, I saw everyone in their swim suits and Diego in small shorts.

"Were you all going to leave without us?" Juan asked sadly.

"Not at all. We were actually waiting for you." Lauren smiled sweetly at him.

"Peudo jugar en la piscina ahorha?" Juan asked me.

"Si. Put your swim shorts on first." I told him.

"Come little man. I'll help you so we can beat Callie to the pool." Elliot took Juan in his arms.

"I'll beat you to the pool first." I smirked then ran up to my room. I took off all my clothes off then put on a dark blue bikini.

I grabbed a towel then ran downstairs to see Elliot and Juan running.

"Run Humphrey." Juan yelled. They both laughed and ran straight outside.

"Haha, you lost." Juan and Elliot both laughed at me.

"Ok. What's my punishment?" I sighed in defeat.

They both looked at each other then back at me with smirks on their faces. I knew exactly what they were going to do.

All of a sudden, I was lifted up from behind. I let out a squeak of surprise when I was spun around.

"Dammit Abbott. Put me down." I screamed.

"As you wish." He laughed then dropped me into the pool.

"Asshole." I shouted before I went under. When I came back up, I saw Juan and Diego laughing which made me smile.

In the end I started laughing with them. "Alright, come on help me up." I put my hand out for Juan.

"I'm not that strong." He pouted.

"Get Humphrey to help. You'll both will me able to help me." I shrugged.

"Fine." They both groaned then came over to me. As soon as I had their hands in mine, I gave one sharp pull and they both fell in the pool.

"Perra." Elliot mumbled.

Juan gasped. "You can't call Callie that."

"What are you gonna do about it little man."

Just then, Juan went up to Elliot and punched him in the arm. With a little bit of my training, Juan got a good hit.

"Ouch. Ok. I'm sorry." Elliot held his arm.

"Pussy." I mumbled.

"Let's party!" Miles and Hendrix both yelled then jumped into the pool with the others following.

"Where's Abbott?" Lauren frowned and looked around.

All of a sudden, there was a loud bang coming from inside the house.

"Stay with Elliot boys. Lauren, Harriette same with you. Boys let's go." I ordered. Me, Grayson, miles and Hendrix all got out of the pool then went inside.

I found Abbott in the living room, sat on the floor with his knees to his chest and shoulders shaking.

The boys gave me small nods then went back outside. I walked over to Abbott and put my hand on his shoulder.

He grabbed my hand, pulling me to the floor and pinning me there while he hovered over me.

His eyes were red and his cheeks were covered in tears.

"What happened?"

Chapter 12. Sleepover II

Joey POV

What happened?" Worry laced my voice as I was trapped underneath Abbott.

"Someone killed my mom." He whispered but I could still hear it cracking.

"Abbott I'm so sorry." I looked up at him.

"You can't tell Lauren. She was close with my mom. She just doesn't know about the gang. She can't know that my mom was killed by my dads rival." Abbott begged.

"Of course. Are you going to tell her?"

"I have to. Just, she can't know how. All she needs to know is that she's gone."

"Abbott?" I looked up at him.

"What?" He said harshly.

A bit of guilt washed over me. But then there was hurt, I was hurt by the way he spoke to me.

"Are you ok?" I asked quietly.

"No." He shook his head. "My mom was all I had. My dad doesn't care about anyone other than himself and that damn gang. Now the most important person to me is gone."

"Do you want me to leave you alone?"

"Yes." He whispered. Abbott let go of me. I got up and went to walk away.

My wrist was grabbed and I was pulled back down, landing on his lap. Abbott buried his face in the crook of my neck and cried.

I moved so I was straddling him so he could hug me. His sobs filled my ears and his tears made my shoulder wet.

After a while, his sobs turned to hiccups as he held me close to his chest. I kept my arms around him so I could give him as much comfort as I could.

"It's all my fault." Abbott whispered.

"How is it?" I asked him.

"I should have been home. Instead she let me come here so I could be a teenager. I was supposed to be protection my mom and she died because she wanted me to be normal." He looked at me.

"It's not your fault. No one knew this would happ-," I started but was cut off by my phone ringing.

I picked it up and tried to sound normal.

"Hello?"

"Is this joey Smith?" A mans voice came through the phone. His voice cracked as he spoke.

"This is she." I replied.

"I need you to kill a man called Connor Benson."

"Of course. May I ask what for?"

"He killed my wife. I want him dead. I can pay you however much you want." The man told me.

I looked at Abbott for a second. "What is your wife's name?"

"Hayley. Hayley stone."

"No pay needed. Just tell me the time and location and I'll be there."

"Are you sure?" He questioned.

"I'm sure." With that, I hung up.

"I'm going to kill the man who murdered your mom." I mumbled.

"My dad called you?" Abbott looked at me with sad eyes.

"Yeah." I whispered. "His name is Connor Benson. He's asked me to kill him as he killed Hayley stone." I told him.

"When is it?" Abbott looked at me. Just then, my phone buzzed letting me know I had a text message.

"Griffith park again. Tomorrow night at 10pm." I read the message.

"I'll be with my dad then. Is it alright if I just go up to a room to be on my own for a while?" He asked me.

"Sure. If you want to get some stress off, I have a shooting range in the basement. It's soundproof so no one will hear you. So it's a room or shoot a dummy?" I laughed a little.

"Thanks Joey. I really mean it."

"Anytime. I'll tell the others your sleeping or something." I stood up.

Abbott went down to the basement while I went back outside to the pool.

"Is he alright?" Grayson asked me, worry lacing his voice.

I shook my head a little then sat down on one of the sun loungers.

"What happened?" Lauren got my attention.

"It's not my place to say. Abbott will tell you later. He's just getting some stress off at the moment." I replied.

"Is he down in the basement?" Elliot said.

"Yeah. It's quiet so it's best if we all leave him alone until he comes to us." I told them.

After a couple hours, the sun went down so we all went inside to get ready for pizza.

Me, Lauren and Harriette were all in shorts and tank tops while all the boys had shorts on. And yes, they were all topless.

"I don't understand boys? Why don't you put tops on?" Harriette furrowed her eyebrows.

"Because it's better. Anyone would agree with me, sleeping in only boxers is amazing." Grayson said in a 'duh' tone.

"I agree. If I was on my own I would either be on my underwear and bra or completely naked." I shrugged.

"You know you can sit in your undies in front of us if you want. We won't do anything." Elliot winked at me.

"Stop being dirty Elliot. It's nasty. Keep your clothes on." Juan looked at me.

"Yes boss." I smiled at him.

Abbott POV

While I was in joeys shooting range, I couldn't help by shout and punch things. Good thing there was a gym here as well.

I spent a lot of time hitting the punching bag and a while shooting a dummy. I could see all the bullet holes from when joey used it last.

After a couple hours, I went back upstairs. It was now dark and I found everyone curled up on the sofas wearing pyjamas. The boys in shorts without a T-shirt, including Juan and Diego. And the girls were in shorts and tank tops.

And my god, did joey look sexy in hers.

Chapter 13. Tears and chick flick

Abbott's POV

"Can we talk for a second?" I quietly asked Lauren.

"Yeah. Is it about earlier? Are you ok?" She moved closer to me. She had a worried expression. Could I tell her that my mom died?

I had a small battle in my head about telling her. She needed to know but there would be so many questions that I wouldn't be able to answer.

"What is it?" Lauren pressed when I didn't answer her.

"This is going to suck because you were close with her." I took a deep breath. "My moms dead."

"What do you mean dead?" She laughed nervously. I could hear it in her voice that she didn't want it to be true.

"My mom died. My dad found her body a couple hours ago." I told her.

"No! No. Tell me this is some sick joke Abbott. Please tell me that your lying." She begged as tears streamed down her face.

I quickly pulled her to my chest. "I'm so sorry Lauren." I held her close to me while she sobbed into my chest.

"Why is Lauren crying?" Diego turned to Joey.

"Someone very close to her died today. She's just grieving." Joey told him.

"Who left?" Juan stood next to his brother in front of Joey.

"Laurens aunt. And Abbott's mom. You know how you feel about mommy?" They both nodded. "That's how Abbott feels, but because she isn't here anymore, it hurts him."

"Why is Lauren sad if it's not her mommy?" Diego looked at me then Lauren while she carried on sobbing into my chest.

"How would you feel if mommy or aunt alma died?"

"Very sad." Both boys said sadly.

"That is how Abbott and Lauren feel. Your to young to understand right now but as you get older you'll get it more." Joey explained to them.

"How can we make Lauren feel better?" Diego hugged Lauren's back.

"Ice cream and a chick flick. How does that sound?" Harriette said.

"Yeah. Let's do this." Lauren pulled away from me. Joey went to get everyone Ben and Jerry's ice cream while I put on, pitch perfect 2.

Diego and Juan cuddled up to Lauren while they watched the movie. Everyone had blankets on them other than me.

I stood up and went over to Joey. I sat next to her and pulled the blanket over me as well. Joey leaned into my side as I put my arm around her.

"Thank you for that." I whispered.

"It's ok. They understand a lot. They get what I do they just don't know how to be when others are upset like that." Joey told me.

"I know. They're so young. I hope they don't lose Gloria so young." I sighed.

"Not while I'm around. That whole family took me in as their own without so much as a second thought. I owe it to them, to protect them all until my last breath."

"How is a cold hearted assassin have such big heart?" I chuckled a little.

"I'm only cold hearted when I kill people. I can't be an asshole in front of those boys. They don't deserve it so I give them a huge smile and things to keep them happy." Joey giggled.

"You're so fucking cute you know that?" I smiled down at her.

"Hmm. Maybe you need to get your eyes tested. I'm not cute, hot or sexy. You need glasses." She laughed a little.

"You're the one who needs glasses then. I can assure you, that you are one sexy girl." I whispered in her ear seductively.

I trailed my spare hand up her legs to her upper thighs. Joey took in a sharp breath as she felt my hand close to her.

"Stop. There's kids here." Joey whispered yelled at me.

We both looked around to see that Diego and Juan were fast asleep with ice cream around their mouths.

Joey stood up and walked over to the sleeping boys and took their ice cream tubs from their hands. She left the room but came back minutes later with a wash cloth.

Joey wiped their mouths and hands carefully so she wouldn't wake them up. Miles, Hendrix and Lauren were all asleep like the kids.

Harriette and Grayson were cuddled up together in their own little world. Once joey was done taking all the ice cream from the others, she sat back down next to me.

"You ok?" I said while kissing her neck.

"Hmm mmm." Joey hummed. "What are you doing?"

"This." I trailed up her neck, kissing her jaw and chin finally up to her lips. Grayson and Harriette didn't say anything. When I looked at them, they were like me and joey.

Slowly, I laid her down and hovered over her. I spread her legs open so I could lay between them. Joey let out a small moan as my semi hard on came in contact with her heat.

"Ah hem." Someone cleared their throat, interrupting us again. Why does everyone interrupt?

We pulled away from each other and looked up. Grayson and Harriette were giving us knowing looks.

"What?" I shrugged while joey giggled hiding her face.

"Nothing. Maybe take it somewhere else. So no little ones get scarred." Grayson chuckled.

"Come on. It was harmless kissing?" I rolled my eyes. I kept myself on top of Joey not caring if my two best friends were looking.

"That's not what it sounded like to me. That was proper make out, tongues and all. Trust me, if we didn't stop you, you would have gone all the way." Harriette smirked.

"Damn, maybe I should have the house to myself more often. That way I can do stuff without being interrupted." Joey said sarcastically.

"This isn't the first time?" Grayson and Harriette gasped dramatically.

"No." Joey blushed and shook her head. "When Abbott went with me to do my job we were caught."

"Wow. We should have just left you. I'm sure Abbott has a bad case of blue balls now." Grayson laughed.

"Yeah I do. It's bad." I sat up, pulling joey up with me.

"Do you have a shower I can use. Sounds great right about now." I whispered to Joey.

"Yeah. You can use the one in my room or there's one in the weapons room." She whispered back so the others couldn't hear.

"I'll go in your one." I winked at her then left.

Chapter 14. Unpaid job

- -

Joey POV

After a long day with Juan and Diego, I dropped them off at the liquor store. Gloria and Miguel were thankful that I took them for the night.

"Can we do it again joey?" Diego made puppy eyes and pouted.

"Of course. But you have to ask your mom and dad before you just jump ahead." I laughed a little.

"Thanks Joey. Bye." Both boys hugged me then went to the back.

"Got a job tonight?" Miguel asked me.

"Yeah."

"How much?"

"Nothing. A man killed Abbott's mom so I was called to kill him. I chose to do it for nothing, I just wanted to do this for my friend." I explained.

"You are a good girl aren't you. Be safe little assassin. I'll see you soon." Miguel hugged me then I left.

Abbott left earlier in the day so he could be with his dad. He wanted to organise the funeral and what the plan was for tonight.

It was now 11pm. I was hidden up high so I had a clear view of the men. Abbott and his dad were talking to each other.

"Hello?" I answered my phone.

"Hey. What time are you going to be home?" Elliots voice came through.

"I don't know. I'm busy at the moment hopefully not long. Why?"

"I have a girl round."

"Ok. I was thinking of staying behind anyway. Just to clear my head. See you in the morning El." I said then hung up.

Another group of me showed up after a while. I could see Abbott's dad walk up to who I assume is Connor Benson.

'Are you here?' Abbott messaged me.

'Always. I got my eye on him so get your dad to do something so I can kill him.'

'On it.'

I watched it all unfold. Abbotts dad pushed Connor and started yelling. All of a sudden, one of Connor's men pulled out a gun.

Of course I was quicker, and his body hit the ground with blood pooling around his head. Connor pulled out a knife and went to stab Abbott's dad but I shot him in the hand then in the head.

I packed up gun then went down to where Abbott's gang was.

Once he saw me, I dropped my bag and ran up to him. My arms went around his neck as my legs wrapped around his torso.

"Thank you so much." Abbott whispered in my ear.

"My pleasure." I laughed a little. I pulled away a little then took off my bandana.

"What ar-," Abbott began but I cut him off by crashing my lips on to his.

After a few minutes, we both pulled away and rested our foreheads on each other's.

"What was that for?" He smirked.

"My oh so huge crush on you came out." I rolled my eyes playfully with a smile.

"Abbott? Who's your friend?" A deep voice said.

Abbott let me down and we both turned to his father. "Dad this is my friend."

"Does she have a name?" The man raised an eyebrow.

"Uh. Yeah but I'd rather, um." Abbott stuttered.

"Joey smith sir." I nodded.

"Your pretty young aren't you? Nice to meet you miss smith. I owe you for doing this for me."

"Don't worry about it. I wanted to do it for Abbott and you. My parents were killed in a car crash. A drunk driver, he's in prison now so I can't kill him. But it was a pleasure to help you." I told him.

"Thank you joey. How old are you anyway?" The man asked.

"18. 19 in a month." I replied.

"Who taught you how to do this?"

"I can't say. He's a cruel man that no one should know about. Sadly me and my friend Elliot had met him." I looked down.

"Well, thank you for your assistance miss smith. Me and my men will keep your face a secret. Glad I can put a face to a name now. Abbott, where are off to?" He looked from me to Abbott.

"I was going to take a walk around here. Clear my head for a couple hours. I'll see you back at the house." He smiled a little.

"Alright." His dad said then walked off. Within minutes, me and Abbott were left on our own.

"What are you doing?" Abbott turned to me, putting his hands on my waist.

"Not much. Elliot has girl over so I was going to stick around til morning. I've decided not to go to school tomorrow." I replied, putting my hands around his neck.

"Want to stay with me? I'd like the company." He smirked.

"I'm not having my first time in a damn national park. I'll stay, just some other time." I laughed.

"I can deal with that. Come on." Abbott laced our fingers and pulled me along. He picked up my bag on the way.

"What happened to your parents?" Abbott broke the silence after a while of walking.

"We were driving. I was asleep in the back of the car and a drunk driver hit them. The car went over a bridge and my parents drowned. They just about got me out. I was in hospital for two months before they told me what happened and put me in an orphanage." I told him.

"I'm sorry you had to go through that."

"I'm not. I barely remember them and the accident. It doesn't matter to me anymore. All I have to do is keep going on with my life. Bad shit happens, even if we don't want it to, it does. We can't do shit about it so why focus on the past when we can look forward into the future." I shrugged.

"You always manage to amaze me Callie Rose." Abbott laughed.

"So do you Abbott stone."

"Good." He smirked then leaned down to kiss me. God what is this guy doing to me?

Chapter 15. Happy birthday

J oey POV

"Happy two months bestie." Lauren shouted down the hall. All of a sudden she ran at me. She jumped on me causing us both to fall the ground.

The students around us had amused yet concerned faces. I smiled sheepishly and shrugged it off.

"What do you mean happy two months?" I asked when Lauren let me up. "You make us sound like a fucking couple."

"Nope. We've known each other for two months. Anyway, we are having celebration drinks tonight. I was hoping it could be at your place." Lauren smiled widely.

"You know I'm always down for drinks with our dorky friendship group. But I have to warn you, I have friends from Chicago coming to see me for a couple days."

"That's cool. We'll have a small party with only us dorks and your friends. And you have enough room so we can crash and stay there. I'd rather not come to school with a hangover."

"You know it's alright with me. I don't have work so I'm all yours tonight." I winked at her.

"Ohh joey. Don't do that. It's a real turn on." Lauren said seductively.

"What are you going on about?" I laughed.

"Damn, I didn't know you rolled that way." Abbott came up behind me.

"Nah I'm straight. But I was just telling Lauren that I was all hers tonight. It's our two months today." I rolled my eyes.

"Can I join in on the action? It's been a while."

"Not with me your not!" Lauren exclaimed. "I've got my hook up for a when I'm drunk anyway."

"Who's that?" I asked.

"Elliot." She giggled.

"Speaking of, he should be here any minute." I told her.

Just then, Elliot walked through the doors. All the girls looked at him, batting their eyelashes. Some of them even pushed up their boobs so they could get his attention.

"Baby!" Lauren shrieked and ran up to him, tackling him to the floor like she did with me. The other girls scoffed and turned away.

"What are you doing tonight?" Abbott whispered in my ear. His hands roamed up the sides of my thighs.

"Drinks with the friend group. We have to celebrate mine and Lauren's two months. But I don't have work so we can drink as much as we want." I bit my bottom lip.

"Sounds good. Just saying, I'm staying in your bed tonight. The one in my room is... uncomfortable without you."

"Nice try big guy." I laughed. "I have friends from Chicago coming to stay with me for a couple days. They are like brothers to me so they are really protective over me. Just a heads up."

"No problem. Maybe I'll take you down to the basement where's it's soundproof." Abbott winked at me.

"I'm not having my first time in a damn basement and who says it's going to be with you?" I raised a questioning brow.

"Me. So what are your brothers like from Chicago?"

"Very similar to Elliot actually. But they're more serious around others but a teddy bear at heart."

"Who's a teddy bear? And happy birthday joey." Elliot came up to us with Lauren, Harriette, Grayson, Hendrix and Miles.

"It's your birthday?" Lauren and Harriette both screamed.

"Yes. Now chill. I think people from fucking Australia heard you." I laughed a little.

"Nonsense. It's now our two month party and your birthday. So suck it up buttercup, happy birthday." Lauren hugged me.

"Happy birthday joey." I got calmly from the others.

"Thanks guys." I smiled.

"Come on Elliot, we need your timetable and locker. Let's go." Lauren dragged him towards the office.

"Has it really been two months since we've all known each other?" I asked in disbelief.

"Well with Lauren's loud ass around, I'm sure it feels longer. Anyway we better get to class. See you later joey." Harriette hugged me then walked away.

Grayson, miles and Hendrix all followed after her like lost puppies.

"Happy birthday." A husky voice whispered in my ear. He has his arms around my waist, keeping my trapped between his chest and arms.

"Thank you. It really isn't my birthday though. It's the date Pablo gave me." I admitted.

"I'm sorry. I can get Lauren to wait until tomorrow or something. I don't want this gorgeous face being upside down today."

"No it's good. I don't have work and I can let loose and get drunk with my new and old friends." I turned around to face him.

"Ok. So what is exactly happening with everyone?" He asked.

"We will all get wasted then crash wherever. I don't care, I just want to be at home and drink until I can't remember my own name. That sounds like a great party to me."

"Whatever you want joey. I won't be drinking though. That way you can drink that much and I can make sure no drunk people go up to your weapons room."

"You don't have to. I'll just lock the door and basement." I shrugged.

"Ok. But i still won't be drinking. I don't feel like it tonight." Abbott chuckled a little.

"Be prepared to babysit a wasted joey then. And I'm counting on you to keep me from blurting out any secrets."

"Of course. Well I'll see you later. I've got to get to class." Abbott pecked my lips before walking away from me.

Damn this boy isn't even my boyfriend yet we act like a couple. Am I falling for my best friends cousin?

Chapter 16. Chicago boys

J oey POV (Landon)

The rest of the school day went by quickly. Elliot seemed to be fitting in well. Other than the girls that wanted him, there were no problems.

Actually, that's a lie. Everywhere Elliot is, there's trouble. On his first day he had a fight with one of football players. Then he was sent to the principals office because he argued with a teacher.

"You are fucked up Elliot." I laughed at him when he came out of the principals office.

"Shut up. He shouldn't have said I was on steroids then. Only if he knew." Elliot said as we got into my car.

"Oh yes. He would be oh so scared of you." I rolled my eyes and started driving. "I doubt he would believe you anyway."

"Whatever.   Let's   just   get   home."
~~~~~~~~~~~~~~~~~~~~~~~~~~~~

Once I parked the car, I saw Lauren, Abbott, Harriette, Grayson, Hendrix and Miles stood at the front door.

"You all ready for par-tay?" Lauren cheered loudly.

"Calm down girl. We got all night for that." I laughed. I unlocked the door and went inside. We all dropped our bags and took off our shoes.

"Wait." I called out.

"You feel it to?" Elliot asked me. I nodded and gestured for the others to be quiet.

I walked quietly round the house to see where people could be. "El, you got eyes on the living room?" I whispered.

"Yeah. No sight."

We eventually got to the games room to see six guys sat on the bar stalls. Like Elliot, I grabbed tennis balls and threw one at each of the guys.

"You guys are such assholes." I tried not to laugh.

"Joey!" They all yelled and pulled me into a group hug.

"I thought you were coming later tonight?" I looked at all of them.

"We wanted to surprise you kiddo. Happy birthday by the way." Graham ruffled my hair.

"Shut up." I swatted his hand away.

"Boys this is abbot, Lauren, Harriette, Grayson, Hendrix and Miles. These are my friends from school." I introduced them.

"Guys this is Graham, Owen, Liam, Mason, Daniel and Sebastian." I added. "These are my friends from Chicago."

"Nice to meet you all." Graham smiled at them.

"Elliot. Fuck me, long time no see." Mason laughed and hugged him.

"Good to see you boys again. I can't believe it's been so long." Elliot smiled.

"What? Two years. Damn it's to long." Sebastian chuckled.

Just then, an older man came through the door. He had dark brown hair with grey showing. His muscles showing through his T-shirt as he flexed.

Tears filled my eyes as I looked at the man standing there. The man that looked after me, cleaned all my wounds and held my while I cried at night.

A few tears fell as i carried on looking at him. "Landon?" I whispered.

"Hello Chiquita." He smiled at me. I didn't hesitate to run into his arms. My legs and arms wrapped around him.

My sobs filled the room as Landon held on to me. I could hear his quiet sniffles while I buried my face in the crook of his neck.

"I thought you were dead. Pablo told me you died last year." I cried.

"I would never leave you Chiquita. I was shot and taken to hospital. Maybe Pablo misunderstood and told you I had died."

"Don't fucking scare me like that again. Your my brother and best friend."

"Nunca. Siempre estaré aquí." Landon tightened his grip on me.

After a few minutes of hugging, Landon let my legs fall and I stood up. Having Landon here was the best birthday gift I could ever have.

"Happy birthday Chiquita." Landon smiled down at me.

"Thanks." I punched his arm playfully. "And where did this come from?" I gripped on to his bushy beard.

"It's called being a man Chiquita. And I have no time to shave since I have a lot of as-,"

"They don't know." I blurted out. "Only Abbott and Elliot know what I do. I'm not ready for the others to know yet."

"Sorry." Landon mumbled. "Anyway, what are we doing birthday girl?"

"I'm staying home and getting wasted until I can't remember my name."

"Are you not working tonight?" Owen asked me.

"Nope. I'm all free. And it's mine and Lauren's two months. As in we've been friends for two months. Her words not mine." I shrugged.

"Right? Well let's get this party started." Lauren, Harriette, Grayson, Hendrix, Miles, Mason, Liam and Graham all cheered.

Chapter 17. Drunk words are sober thoughts

A bbott POV

After joey was done catching up with her friends from Chicago, we all started drinking. Unlike the other times, Joey didn't hold back.

She was dancing on the pool table and drinking shots like they were water. I had got to know the boys, they told me stories about joey and she told me some about them.

"Dude do you remember when owen was caught jerking off in the shower? The look on his face was brilliant." Joey burst out laughing.

"It's not funny. I was horny and it's all I could do. Landon and Elliot never let any of us go near you." Owen whined.

"Yes because I know there's someone better out there for joey. And that person is not you." Landon laughed.

"If there is anyone in this room that you could choose for joey, who would it be and why?" Daniel asked Landon.

Landon looked at me and smiled. "None of you. No one will be good enough for my Chiquita and she will be single for the rest of my life if I have anything to say about it."

"Did you see the way he looked at you?" Miles whispered to me.

"I have no idea what you are doing on about." I smirked at him.

As the night went on, everyone got more and more drunk. At around 11pm, Grayson and Harriette went up to the room they always share.

"Use protection guys." Joey slurred as they walked up the stairs.

"I'm on the pill so it doesn't matter." Harriette winked. We all heard Harriette giggle then their bedroom door slam shut.

"I have work soon so I better go to my room." Landon stood up.

"Same here." Owen, Daniel, Sebastian, Graham, Liam and mason all agreed.

"What do you guys work as?" Lauren slurred.

"Relators. We have to show houses and it's a long day tomorrow. Come along boys, goodnight all." Landon replied then walked off. The others following by his orders.

"You want to come to my room?" Elliot drunkly smirked at Lauren.

"Don't mind if I do." She chugged the last of her beer then followed Elliot up the stairs.

"Are you going to leave me to?" Joey slurred and moved closer to me.

"I can stay if you want me to." I turned to her.

"Them boys don't know how to stay up past midnight. I love them all but they are so boring."

"Maybe it's time you get to bed." I said and took the bottle of vodka from her.

"No!" She exclaimed. "I want to have fun. Come on Abbott, don't be a party pooper."

"You will have a bad hangover tomorrow. I think you should stop and sleep it off." I told her.

"Fine. You owe me big time." Joey pointed at me. She stood up and swayed a little before falling on her ass.

"Come on princess. Let's get you to bed." I said and lifted her up. She wrapped her arms around my neck and clung to me like a koala bear.

"I love you Abbott. Did you know that?" Joey mumbled against my neck. She started laying pepper kisses between my neck and shoulder.

"That day in the halls at school when I first saw you, you made me feels things no one ever has. Not one guy I have met has made me feel things like you do." She added.

"You make me feel things as well joey." I smiled to myself.

"Happy birthday to me, happy birthday to me, happy birthday to me, happy birthday to me." She sang and laughed.

"Yeah joey, happy birthday." I chuckled.

"Abbott will anyone ever love me?" Joey asked as I laid her down in her bed.

"Of course joey. Anyone guy would be lucky to have you as theirs. You'll find someone someday." I smiled at her.

"I love you Abbott."

"I love you to Joey."

"Lay with me. I don't want to be on my own anymore." Joey pulled my hand so I laid down next to her.

"What do you mean? Anymore?" I wrapped my arms around her and pulled her so her back was against my chest.

"This big house, it gets so lonely. I have no one. Landon and the boys all live in Chicago and I'm here. Elliot goes between each place but is mostly in Chicago. I used to have them all when I was with Pablo then I had Gloria and the boys and now, now I'm on my own." Joey started crying.

"Your not on your own Joey. You have me, Lauren, Harriette, Grayson, Hendrix and Miles. We'll all be here when you need us." I held her tightly.

"Why do you still care about me? I kill people for a living and don't care. And here you are holding me because I'm an emotional drunk." Joey laughed a little.

"I've killed people before. The first man I killed was someone called Lucas Moore. He was doing a weapon deal with my dad, it went wrong and everyone was killed in his gang. Lucas was tortured until I was taken down to the cells." I admitted.

"My dad placed a gun in my hand and told me to shoot him in the head. Lucas begged me not to do it. But I was threatened by my dad and I was left no choice but to shoot him." I told her.

"How old were you when that happened?" Joey turned to face me. Our faces were really close, I could smell the bourbon in her breath.

"14. I was fourteen years old when I killed him."

"I was thirteen. Pablo was so harsh on us and we were beat at least once a week. That's how I get by. I remember what Pablo did to me and I use that anger to help me."

"Joey we are the same. No one will understand us but we get each other. But I promise you that you'll have me, as a friend any time you need me." I hugged her tightly.

"I'll be here for you. Night Abbott, I'll see you in the morning." Joey kissed my cheek then snuggles into my chest.

"Night Joey." I smiled to myself then go to sleep.

This is going to be so fun telling her in the morning. She's a funny drunk but gets deep. Not only is Joey smart and beautiful, but she is broken. From a young age she has been through a lot.

Everyone goes through something in life, but Joey was made into something she isn't. Not only is she fragile, she is a child at heart. Joey never got the love and affection I got. All she got was a fist to the face and told what to do.

That is going to change. I will show Joey love and I will do it unconditionally. Nothing will get in my way of loving Joey smith.

Chapter 18. Hangover and confessions

J oey POV

I woke up to a pounding in my head. My eyes hurt and my head felt like I was being hit by a hammer.

When I got downstairs, I was greeted by a groaning Lauren and a dead looking Harriette. All the boys looked fine.

"How the fuck are you all not hungover?" I whispered to the boys.

"Because we're not alcoholics like you girls." Owen shouted.

"Don't yell brother. My head hurts to much." I whined and sat down next to the girls.

"Never will I drink like that again." Lauren mumbled.

"Never will I drink with joey. You crazy ass." Harriette rubbed her temples.

"Don't blame me. You both joined me whenever I took a shot you both told me to do you one as well." I narrowed my eyes at them.

"Drink this." Landon passed us all glasses.

"What's this?" Harriette picked you the glass and looked at it.

"Hangover remedy. Just drink it and you'll feel better soon. It's better than taking Advil. Now drink up ladies, I don't have all day." Landon clapped his hands.

"Dick." I muttered then started chugging the drink. Once I was done, I put the glass down and gagged. "I think I'd rather of had Advil."

"Suck it up Chiquita. Now I have to go. I'll be back later. Laters joey." Landon kissed the top of my head then left.

"We're off as well. See you later joey. And we are using a car. I left mine at home so I'm going to take the green Tesla. Bye joey." Owen winked at me then left.

Daniel, Graham, Sebastian, Liam and mason all followed Owen to the garage to take a car.

"Hang on. I saw your car parked out front." I frowned at Sebastian.

"Sugar I know. You just have better cars than me. And I want to use that dark blue lambo of yours." Sebastian smirked then left.

"My head still hurts." I groaned and put my head on the counter.

"Here." Abbott chuckled. He put a glass of water and two Advil in front of me.

"Thanks. What would I do without you guys." I smiled then took the Advil, downing all the water.

"Well I better get home. My mom is literally going to kill me." Lauren sighed. "Actually, I cant deal with her today. I have a headache and I want to sleep. I'll be in my room."

Lauren yawned then got up and went upstairs. "I agree. I'm going to sleep as well." Harriette stood then walked away.

"We better get home. See you later guys." Hendrix and miles smiled at me then left. Now it was just me, Abbott Grayson and Elliot.

"What happened last night?" I asked.

"You were so funny. You were dancing on the pool table and drinking a shot every five minutes." Elliot laughed.

"It was amazing. I expected you to be calm and all. You were a total wild card." Grayson smirked.

"God. What didn't I do last night?" I whined.

"Get laid?" Elliot shrugged.

"Well I wasn't naked this morning and I was alone so I guess I wasn't as lucky as your two."

"That's a win. Anyway I better go check on Harriette." Grayson sighed then left.

"I better go to Lauren. Before she has a bitch fit." Elliot laughed then followed Grayson up the stairs. I could hear them both joking about the hungover girls in their rooms.

"What was I like last night?" I broke the silence between me and Abbott.

"Want me to lie or tell the truth?" He looked down.

"The truth." I replied.

"At around 11pm everyone went up to bed and it was just you and me. I had to take a bottle of vodka from you so I could get you to bed. Then you cried and said your were lonely." Abbott confessed.

"Is that all?" I hoped it was.

"That was something else but I don't think you want to hear it."

"Please tell me. This is so embarrassing."

"You randomly said you loved me. Started kissing my neck when I carried you to bed. Then you had a break down." Abbott told me.

"Seriously?" I asked.

"Yeah. Don't worry though, you were drunk and didn't mean it. It's ok joey." He laughed but I could hear the nervousness behind it.

But the thing was I really did. I did love Abbott. He's helped me get through a lot. It broke my heart to see him when he cried about his mom, it made me smile when he would smile at me. And the butterflies in my stomach when we would hug or the way my heart would flutter when he would make comments to me.

I love Abbott stone. Ever since I saw him on my first day at school. But I can't, Pablo would kill him. I'm in love with Abbott stone and I won't stop.

"Abbott." I whispered.

"Yeah?" He answered.

"I was telling the truth last night. I really do love you." I admitted.

All of a sudden, Abbott pulled me into his arms and kissed me. It wasn't forced but rough and filled with love.

"Good because I love you as well." He mumbled against my lips then went back to kissing me.

Chapter 19. I'll be yours

Joey POV (mature content)

We both stood in the middle of the kitchen heavily making out. I wanted more, I needed more.

"Be mine." Abbott breathed out when he pulled back.

"I'll be yours." I smiled.

Abbott didn't waste time crashing his lips to mine again. His hands went to my thighs and lifted me up. My legs wrapped around his torso as he carried me up the stairs.

After a couple minutes, we got to my room. Abbott shut the door and pushed me against it. He locked the door while he kissed down my neck.

"Abbott." I moaned.

"Joey." He groaned against my neck.

I pulled his T-shirt over his head and threw in over his shoulder. I started grinding on his hard shaft.

"Fuck joey." Abbott moaned in my ear.

"I want you Abbott. I need you." I whispered to him.

"Are you sure?" He looked at me. All I could see was love and lust in his eyes. It was in that moment I realised, he was it for me.

"Yes. I want it to be with you."

"I'll be gentle I promise." He told me then kissed me affectionately.

I felt my back being taken away from the door and placed on a soft surface. Abbott hovered over me, spreading my legs with his knees.

His kisses trailed down my neck and over my shoulder to my collar bone. Abbott lifted me up a little and took off my T-shirt I was wearing.

As soon as my T-shirt was off, me leaned me down and started kissing from my throat to my stomach.

My breathing got quicker as he started grinding on me. His hard shaft came in contact with my aching heat making me moan breathlessly.

My hands went down to his pants and took off his belt causing it to make a loud thud on the floor. Soon, his pants followed, leaving him only in his boxers.

Abbott didn't hesitate to take off my pants and throw them on the floor with all the other clothes.

"Good thing everyone is busy now. It would have been hard to do this with everyone around." Abbott mumbled against my neck.

"Hmm mm. Landon especially wouldn't let me out of his sight." I breathed out.

"I love you joey. To goddamn much."

"I love you to Abbott. More than you know." I moaned.

He lifted me up again and took off my bra. My arms went around me so I could cover myself. It felt weird doing this. To be honest, I had never been touched by a man in this way.

"Don't hide yourself from me joey. You're beautiful in my eyes." Abbott moved my arms from covering me and laid me back down.

"Abbott, no one has ever done this to me before. I've never been touched by a guy before." I moved my face so he couldn't see my red cheeks.

I felt his hand go under my chin and move me so we were looking at each other again. "I'll take it easy on you. If you want me to stop, I'll stop. If you want me to go on, I'll do it. We'll go at your own pace, it's worth the wait."

"Will it hurt?" I asked nervously.

"Yes but it'll pass. I promise you I'll make sure you'll be ok." He reassured me.

"Ok. I want this. I want you." I looked up at him.

He nodded and kissed me lovingly. It wasn't fast or forced, he was willing to take things slow with me.

His warm hands went down my sides and his fingers played with my underwear. Just then, he pulled them off me so the only thing that was in between us now was his boxers.

I shuddered a little from the coldness of the room. From being clothed to completely naked, it took its toll on me.

"Get under the sheets. It'll be better and you won't be as cold." Abbott smiled at me. We both got under and went back to heavily making out.

I pulled down his boxers and he kicked them off somewhere on the bed. There was no going back. I wanted Abbott and he wanted me. He made me feel loved. There was no way I could repay him for how he makes me feel.

Abbott picked my one of my legs and put it so it was around his waist. He looked at me with his sexy blue eyes and swollen lips.

"Hang on." He muttered then leaned over the bed. He pulled up his pants and took out his wallet. Abbott then dropped his wallet on the floor and showing me a condom.

"I'm sure you don't want to be a mom anytime soon. And I want to wait to be a dad." He chuckled.

"I agree. I can barely look after myself let alone another human." I giggled.

Abbott ripped the wrapper with his teeth then pulled the condom over his very erect length.

He positioned himself on top of me again, pulling my leg over his waist again. I could feel his length at my entrance.

"Abbott." I said with worry lacing my voice.

"Baby if you don't want to then we won't." He caressed my cheek.

"I want to I'm just scared. It's all new to me." I told him.

"I know. Just tell me when it gets to much and I'll stop." He said. I nodded and he bent down and kissed me. It took my mind off it for a while.

I felt Abbott lower his hips and the tip of him enter me. I winced in pain a little. He captured my lips and kissed me like the first time we did it.

I could still feel him going into me, but it wasn't that bad. It still hurt but I was more focused on the kiss. After a few minutes, I felt the base of him.

"Are you ok?" Abbott kissed me softly on the nose.

"Yeah. Just a little weird." I replied.

"Can I start moving?" He kissed me once more. I nodded and closed my eyes for the pain.

Abbott pulled back, almost leaving me, but then he thrusted back into me. A loud moan left my lips as he went in and out over and over again.

"Fuck." Abbott groaned and closed his eyes. "Damn baby girl your so good. Shit."

"Abbott." I moaned. "Faster."

Abbott picked up the pace, as he got faster, his thrusts got harder. I bit my bottom lip to keep in the moans but it didn't work.

A knot formed in my stomach making me want Abbott to go faster. Like reading my thoughts, Abbott went even faster, both our groans mixed together as he pounded into me.

"Cum for me baby girl. I've got you." Abbott breathed out. I felt myself let lose as I came. Abbott stopped moving so I guessed he climaxed like me.

He thrusted into me a few more times before laying next to me. Abbott pulled the full condom from himself and threw it in the trash can beside my bed.

"How do you feel?" He asked me. I could heard the worry in his voice as he touched my cheek.

"Fine. That was amazing." I gave him a tight lipped smile.

"Let's take a shower then clean the bed." He pecked my lips then lifted me from the bed.

When I looked down, there was blood on the white sheets. "I'm not on my period." I whispered.

"I know. It's ok, it's normal for that to happen. Don't worry about it. We can have a shower then change the bed. I'll go wash it once we're done." Abbott held me close to him.

"Can we have a bath instead?" I asked.

"Whatever you want baby." He kissed my cheek.

Chapter 20. You and me... always

A bbott POV

  I picked up joey and took her into the bathroom. She wouldn't let go of me so I kneeled down with her on my lap, while I filled the bath tub up with bubbles.

Once it was full, I stood up and got in. Joey still clung to me, like she never wanted to let go of me.

"Will you ever leave me?" She whispered.

"Never. I'll be here for as long as you want me to." I kissed her head. "It's you and me... always."

"Always?" She looked up at me with hope in her eyes.

"Always." I kissed her. "Maybe always will be our forever."

"You've seen the fault in our stars?" Joey asked in disbelief.

"Lauren and Harriette made us guys watch it. That kind of stuck with me." I replied.

"Maybe we can watch it later when everyone is more alive."

"Anything for you." I kissed the top of her head. "Are you hurting?"

"A little sore but I'll be fine. Nothing a nap won't fix." Joey smiled tiredly.

"Let's get you cleaned up then you can sleep." I pecked her lips then washed her body.

Once I was done, I stood up with joey still clinging on to me. I wrapped a towel around her small frame and one around my waist.

"Baby you'll have to get down so I can change the sheets." I told her.

"Ok." She sighed. I laid her down on the sofa she had in her room so she would be comfortable for a while.

Once I took off the dirty sheets and replaced them with clean ones, I laid joey in the bed.

"Don't leave." She grabbed my hand.

"I'm only doing to put these on to be cleaned. I'll be back in five." I leaned down to kiss her then left.

I picked up our clothes from the floor as well so they could be cleaned. Once I got to the laundry room, I put the sheets in first so no one would question anything.

I threw our clothes in a basket then went back up to Joey. She was curled up in a ball shivering as she laid on top of the covers.

I took off the towel then got under the covers, pulling joey in with me. She positioned herself so she was chest to chest with me.

I put my arm under her head as she snuggled into my chest. I ran my fingers up and down her back. Joey shivered a little and cuddled closer to me.

"Are you ok?" I whispered to her.

"Yeah. I just want to sleep." She closed her eyes and buried her face into my chest and pillow.

"Sleep then. I won't go anywhere." I told her. She mumbled a thank you then went to sleep.

I couldn't help but watch joey. She is definitely something else. There was no doubt that Joey could put a smile on my face without even trying.

"Wakey, wakey love birds." Someone slammed the door open and walked in.

"Awww, look at them." I heard Lauren.

"Are they naked or just topless?" Hendrix asked.

"Oh. My. GOD!" Harriette and Lauren shrieked.

"Shut up I'm trying to sleep." Joey groaned and moved closer to me. My arms went around her as we laid on our sides.

"Our baby's no longer a baby anymore." Elliot sniffled.

I opened one eye to see him actually crying. "Don't cry you pussy. Imagine if pablo saw you." Joey mumbled.

"Shut up. If I want to cry I can. Now get up so we can do something." Elliot wiped his eyes then slapped joeys leg.

"Fuck off. I'm sore and tired. Just leave me alone." Joey argued.

"Babe it's four in the afternoon. We should get up, get some food as well." I yawned.

"Ok." She stretched. I made sure the covers didn't fall down so all the guys could see.

"We'll Wait for you downstairs. I'll order pizza as well so you don't have to cook." Harriette smiled a little then left.

Grayson, miles and Hendrix followed her out, leaving me, Joey, Lauren and Elliot alone.

"What do you want?" Joey looked at them.

"Not much. Making sure you don't do anything else." Lauren shrugged.

"What makes you think we did anything? We could literally be cuddling in bed." I shrugged.

"We don't. I just pieced it together. I mean you're both naked and joey said she's sore. I'm pretty sure that means you took her virginity." Lauren said and Elliot agreed.

"Of course you would agree. Well get out, I don't really want to be seen naked by my cousin and friend." I shooed then out with my hand.

"Fine. But if your not ready in five minutes I'll come back and drag you down myself." Lauren huffed then walked away.

"Better be quick." Elliot winked at us then left, closing the door behind him.

"Come on. I'll carry you if you want." I turned to Joey.

She hummed then nodded. "I'll get some clothes for you." I pecked her lips and got up.

I put on spare boxers and joggers I had left here. I ended up getting shorts and a tank top for joey.

She slipped on underwear, her shorts and the tank top with padding built in. Once joey was dressed, she put her arms out to me. I picked her up so her legs wrapped around my torso.

"Finally. I thought I was going to have to talk in on some live porn or something." Lauren said dramatically.

"Shut up Lauren. Look how cute they look." Hendrix slapped her shoulder.

"I know. My baby cousin has grown up." Lauren wipes away a fake tear.

Chapter 21. Couch cuddling

Joey POV

"I got pizza so we can watch a movie as well." Harriette said.

"Ok, let's go then. I can pay." Abbott announced. He followed everyone into the theatre I have. I didn't move at all, so I was there clinging to him like a damn koala.

"What are we watching then?" Grayson asked as he sat down.

"The fault in our stars." I whispered knowing Abbott would hear me and tell the others.

"Joey want to watch the Fault in our stars." Abbott grabbed the control from Lauren and put it on.

"I'll get it." Abbott said when the doorbell rang.

"No. I don't want to move." I whined.

"I'll go." Elliot said. Abbott gave him the money and he left.

"Seven boxes Harriette? Do we really need this much?" Elliot asked her in disbelief.

"Well yeah. I don't know when the Chicago boys will be back. And the boys here are damn pigs so I thought seven boxes would be enough." She shrugged.

All of a sudden, the front door slammed open. Landon, owen, Daniel, Graham, Liam, mason and Sebastian all came through.

"Fuck this hurts." I heard owen groan in pain.

"What happened?" I sat up in Abbott's lap.

"I got shot, what else does it look like?" Owen squeezed his eyes shut.

"Joey we need your help. Since we have no idea how to do this." Landon said.

"Fine." I rolled my eyes then got up. I took owen from the boys and into the kitchen. "Sit your ass down you big baby."

"Have you ever been shot?" Owen exclaimed.

"No because I know how to do my job properly." I snapped while getting the stuff.

"What job is that?" I heard Hendrix ask. I turned around to see everyone stood by the door.

"Nothing. Owen will be fine when I get the bullet out." I replied. I set all the stuff down and took off his T-shirt.

I got the bullet out with Owen saying a string of curses. It was difficult to stitch up the wound with Owen flinching every two seconds.

"Stay the fuck still." I snapped at him.

"Sorry." He muttered then tried to stay still.

"Jace can fucking do this without moving an inch. Get a grip." I told him.

"Jace is a fucking psycho. But I still feel bad for him." Owen replied.

"So do I." I sighed. I finished stitching the wound then wrapped it up. "There you go. Now get out of my sight."

"Thanks Joey." Owen hugged me then quickly left.

"How did you do that?" Lauren asked me looking astonished.

"A lot of practice. Takes the piss when he can't stay the fuck still." I said as I collected all the equipment up.

"How did he get shot? Surely it wasn't random." Grayson asked.

"Don't worry about it. Owen is irresponsible and can't do his job properly. Now let's get food because I'm hungry." I changed the subject.

"I'm sure you are after this morning." Elliot laughed. Everyone went back into the theatre room.

I sat down with Abbott as we shared a large cheese pizza.

"Baby who's Jace?" Abbott asked me.

"A friend from England. His story is quiet sad actually." I admitted.

"What is it?"

"When he was growing up he was beat by his parents. Once he was fourteen he joined Emilio Di'Angelo's gang. He is well known all over the world. Then he met cora at sixteen. They hit it off and acted like an old married couple. After a month of being together they found out cora was pregnant, had twins but their story ended quickly. Cora was kidnapped when her kids were one years old, she was stabbed and died in Jace's arms. He kissed her goodbye. He left the gang to raise his kids and adopted son while he works in a garage fixing cars and shit. He never took another girlfriend. Even 15 years later he never took another and only focus's on him and his family." I told him.

"How old is he now?"

"Hes 32. His son and daughter are 16. He has a huge family but are kind. No matter what though, don't get on their bad side." I giggled.

"Noted." Abbott nodded then went back to eating and watching the movie.

When it got dark, Landon, Owen, Sebastian, Daniel, Mason, Liam and Graham went to their rooms.

Me and Abbott we're laying on a cuddle chair, Lauren and Elliot on another, Grayson and Harriette on another. Hendrix and Miles both sat on a bean bag since they didn't have girlfriends to be with.

"Don't you guys have girlfriends?" Elliot asked them.

"Nope. We have other... matters to attend to." Miles said like he was hiding something.

"Not only that, but no one at school is likeable. They're so bitchy and I'd be inside her 24/7 so, no we don't have girlfriends." Hendrix shrugged.

"I know someone from England that would like you. She's actually coming here for a while with her family. Why don't you hang around and meet them, they'll be here tomorrow so I won't be at school." I suggested.

"Is she hot?" Miles asked.

"It's not all about looks dick." Hendrix scolded his brother.

"They are. Both are pretty and kind, unlike her father." I told them.

"Awesome. I don't want to go to school anyway. I'll hang around." Miles said.

"Me to." Everyone else agreed. "I don't mind staying here for another night, we can make the most of it." Grayson said.

Everyone chose to put on the walking dead. Me and Abbott were cuddled up, he had his arms around me as I laid on my back.

"What you thinking about?" Abbott kissed my forehead, nose then lips.

"My friends from England. I haven't seen them in a while so I don't know what they're like." I sighed.

"We'll all be here. Not to mention the boys will have your back as well. Don't think to much about it." He pecked my lips.

"I won't." I smiled at him.

"I love you."

"I love you to." I leaned up and kissed him.

"Awww, you two should definitely be a couple." Harriette and Lauren squealed.

"How do you know we aren't already?" Abbott smirked.

"OH. MY. GOD!!" They both yelled.

Chapter 22. England gang

J oey POV

I was woken up with the front door slamming open. "Joey where is your cute arse." A very familiar British accent filled my ears.

"Beks." I squealed then ran to her. When I got to the front door, her arms were out wide and I ran up to her embrace.

"I missed you." Rebekah hugged me tightly.

"I missed you to." I smiled.

"What about us?" More family accents filled my ears.

"Hey guys." I hugged Kieran, Arorah, Mitch, Mikey, max and Lola.

"Damn it's nice to be back here." Rebekah sighed with a smile and took off her sunglasses.

"Good to have you here. Chicago lot are upstairs." I told them. "Is it only you guys?"

Before anyone could reply, a man let out a series of curses. "Fuck. Damn these are heavy."

He walked in and dropped everyone's luggage on the floor.

"You kids are useless. Especially you three, I'm not taking these fucking bags anymore." The black haired man grunted.

"Alright Damon? How's it going?" I smiled.

"Fucking brilliant. Come here, how's my favourite pequeño asesino?" Damon hugged me.

"I'm good. But we have to be quiet since I have my friends in the living room."

"That's ok. We can be silent for as long as they need." Rebekah said.

"Damn brits are so loud. Shut the fuck up." Landon said. He came down the stairs followed by Owen, Sebastian, Graham, Mason, Liam and daniel.

"Fuck me you look good Landon." Damon laughed.

"Looks like your the babysitter for a bunch of teens." Landon rolled his eyes.

"Not just me. I got jace, rose, Salvatore and Emilio in the car. They just have to wake up." Damon shrugged.

When he said that, I ran out of the house to see all of them getting out of the car. I ran up to rose, wrapping my arms around her.

"Hello darling. It's been to long." Rose hugged me tightly.

"I missed you so much." I sniffled.

"Hey, don't be crying. I'll always be here when you need me. Wether it's in England or here. I'm just a phone call away." Rose wiped my eyes.

"I know. Thank you for coming." I smiled.

"No problem. Emilio has beks to look out for, Jace for the twins and Mitch, then me and Salvatore for all of them." She laughed.

"Can never rely on any of them can you?" I chuckled.

I gave everyone hugs when we walked back into my house. We went into the kitchen so we wouldn't wake up the others in the living room.

After half an hour, miles walked into the kitchen. He didn't take any notice of the massive group of people.

"Morning Miles. How'd you sleep?" I asked.

"Not bad. I should have used the room. That bean bag is so uncomfortable." He games and took out a glass and orange juice.

When he turned around he almost dropped everything in his hands. "Hello."

"Hey." Everyone waved.

"Miles this is the people from England. They'll be staying for a couple days." I told him.

"Hi. I'm Miles Montgomery." He smiled shyly.

"Hey. I'm rose. This is my husband Salvatore, son Emilio and his daughter Rebekah. My son in law Damon, he's got a wife and sons at home. Then there's jace and his kids Arorah, Mitch and Kieran and my other sons children, max, mikey and Lola." Rose smiled warmly at him.

"How many more of you are there?" Miles asked astonished.

"You should be glad everyone isn't here." I patted his shoulder.

"Must be a lot then."

"Hell yes." Beks cheered.

"Shut it beks. There's people sleeping, I'd rather not have angry Americans down my throat." Mitch scolded her.

"Whatever." Rebekah rolled her eyes.

A few minutes later, Abbott walked into the kitchen and pecked my lips before getting a drink.

"Nice to meet you all, you must be joeys family from England." Abbott smiled at them.

"Yeah. This is Abbott my boyfriend. Abbott this is rose, Salvatore, Jace, Mitch, Arorah, Kieran, Damon, Emilio, max, mikey, and Lola." I told him.

"He's nice isn't he." Rose winked at me.

"He is. So how come it's only you guys? Where's Luna, willow and the others?" I asked.

"Wanted to stay home so they could watch the-," Salvatore started then stopped when he looked at Miles.

"I get it. The only one here that knows about me is Abbott. Everyone else doesn't know until I want them to." I sighed.

"Have you heard from pablo at all?" Rose asked, worry in her face.

"He came here when Elliot first got here. He left though. I don't know what he's planning or doing but I know he won't stop until he gets me back." I admitted.

"We won't let that happen." Abbott kissed the top of my head.

"Hold up a minute. Did you say Elliot's here?" Arorah asked me.

"Yeah, why?" I laughed, knowing exactly what's about to go down.

"Humphrey Addams get your American arse in here now." Arorah yelled.

Elliot came in rubbing his eyes. Arorah stalked up to him then kicked him in the manhood and punched him in the face.

"That was for last time you prick." She glared at him. "Lovely to see you again."

"What happened last time?" Miles asked me with wide eyes.

"You don't want to know." I shook my head.

"We better go. See everyone later." Landon said.

"Owen don't get shot again or I'll do it myself." I warned him.

"Wouldn't dream of it joey." He gulped then left with all the other Chicago boys.

"Why is everyone so loud so early?" Lauren came in with Harriette.

"Ahhh." Rebekah screamed. "More girls." She squealed then ran up to them and hugging them.

"Hey, I'm Lauren." She said nervously.

"And I'm Harriette." They both introduced themselves.

"Ignore her girls. Beks step away from them before you kill them with your perfume." Mitch smirked while he had one arm around Arorah.

"I will put a bullet through your head Mitch. Trust me I will." Rebekah threatened.

"Rebekah Anne Di'Angelo." Emilio shouted. "Don't use that language while joeys friends are present. Get a grip girl."

"Sorry dad." She rolled her eyes.

"I wish your mother was here." Emilio whined.

"She's got to help aunt Luna, daks and the others." Rose shrugged. "That's why I came."

"When did we go to England?" Lauren said confusedly.

Chapter 23. Eveyone knows

Lauren POV

"When did we go to England?" I asked confusedly.

"We're not in England dumbass. This is joeys family from there." Abbott rolled his eyes.

"Shut up. Not my fault I woke up and had a bunch of British people here."

"Just stop both of you. We better get ready for school anyway." Joey said. She stood up and left with Abbott.

"We better go to Lauren. Nice to meet everyone." Harriette smiled at them then we walked away.

We woke Hendrix up as well and was followed up stairs by both Hendrix and Miles.

"Is everyone ready to leave?" I heard joey shout.

"Yeah." I ran downstairs. We all left in our own cars. Joey was with Abbott, Harriette and Grayson. Miles and Hendrix took one car while me and Elliot went on our own.

When I parked the car at school, I got out and was immediately pushed against the hardness of the car.

"I remember you pretty one." I deep voice whispered in my ear. I could feel their warm breath on my neck.

I felt a pinch of pain in my arm and my eyes go fuzzy. "Night, night Amiga of joeys." Was the last thing I heard before I completely blacked out.

Joey POV

"Where's Lauren? She's usually here by now." Harriette muttered.

"Did she go back home before she came here?" Abbott asked.

"No. Lauren is one to avoid being at home. Because of her parents drinking and all, she usually spends as much time away as she can." Harriette told us.

Just then, my phone started ringing. "Hello." I answered.

"If you wish to see your precious Lauren again, come to base and bring me $5.6 million." Pablos voice came through.

"Don't you fucking touch her pablo. I swear to god I will kill you myself if you harm her." I spat trough the phone.

"Come, come joey. If you bring the money, I'll let her go. If you fail then I will kill this innocent gem." Pablo smirked. I didn't have to see him to know what he was doing.

"H-help m-me joey." I heard Lauren cry out.

"Times ticking little assassin." Pablo said darkly then hung up.

"What's wrong?" Abbott looked worried as he held on to my shoulders.

"Pablo has Lauren." I whispered.

"Shit." He closed his eyes.

"We need to go get her. No more secrets. Everything comes out today." I said loud enough for everyone to hear.

"What secrets? Where's Lauren?" Harriette asked with a shaky voice.

"Meet me back at my house. I'll explain everything there. I'll pay off the school for the amount of days off we've had. Let's go." I ordered then ran out of the school.

Everyone got into their cars and sped off towards my house. Once we got there, I found the England gang in the theatre watching a movie.

"Que pasó?" Rose said when she saw my worried expression. Everyone ran into the house and stood behind me.

"Lauren was taken by Pablo. We need to get her back." I replied.

Jace, Emilio, Salvatore, Mitch and rose all stood up. "What should we do?" Jace asked.

"Follow me." I said. Elliot, Abbott, Grayson, Hendrix and Miles, Jace, Emilio, Mitch, Salvatore and rose all followed me upstairs.

"Gear up. Take as much as you want. I want to kill pablo then get Lauren out carefully. He will have men there so kill anyone that tries to stop you from getting to her." I ordered.

"What is this?" Harriette questioned me with tears in her eyes.

"I'm a trained assassin. I kill people for a living. The Chicago boys are like me, Abbott is in a gang same with the England guys." I explained quickly.

"What the hell?" She breathed out.

"I'll explain more when I get back. Just trust me on this one." I looked at her.

"Ok. Just get my best friend back please." She begged.

"We will try our best. Sometimes they don't get to come back. Just trust us and only time will tell." Jace told her.

"Yeah." Harriette whispered then left.

"How does joey have nicer guns than boss? This is crazy." Grayson laughed.

"What are you talking about?" I chuckled at them.

"We knew. I actually heard you telling your story to Abbott. Then I had to listen to them two fight about how you could have so much money." He shrugged.

"And you still want to be my friend?" I asked.

"Well yeah. We're not ones to judge. We are in Abbott's dads gang. We just didn't go that day when you were told to kill Connor." Miles told me.

"Perfect. Is everyone ready because I am in real need for a good brawl." Emilio smirked.

"Damn kids a fucking psycho." Rose mumbled.

"Mum, you know how I am. Let's get one thing straight, Jace is worse than me. Even Damon agrees." Emilio argued.

"Instead of having a bitch fit Emilio, can we go and save joeys friend. Get a fucking grip come on." Jace rolled his eyes then walked away.

"Everyone got a gun?" I asked. I got a series of 'yea' then we all walked downstairs.

"Be safe. I don't want my boyfriend and dad dead just yet." Arorah hugged Jace and Mitch.

"We'll be fine darling. It's not the first time I've done this. Just make sure you and everyone here is safe, alright?" Jace told her. Arorah nodded then spoke with Mitch.

"Be careful dad. I don't want mum to find out that you got shot on your first day here." Rebekah hugged Emilio.

"I will. Remember everything I've taught you so keep safe. I'd rather have everyone go back home in tact." Emilio chuckled.

"Guess who's here bitches." My front door slammed open.

"Don't look so glum baby face. I've come to see my favourite assassin. So where's Landon?" He asked.

"I thought you were staying at home with your mum and Rosalee?" Damon asked him.

"Dearest father I have come to visit dear old joey and her fancy American home. Now why do you all have guns?"

"Elijah, we're going to save my friend from pablo. Now go get a gun and get your ass in gear." Elliot glared at him.

"Yes!" Elijah cheered. "We're finally going to kill that bastard once and for all." He said then ran up the stairs.

Elijah came back minutes later with a gun in his hand. "Let's go kill some Español arse."

Chapter 24. Goodbye

Lauren POV

I woke up in a small room. My hands and feet were tied to a chair and I had a gag in my mouth.

"Happy to see your awake Lauren. How about we get down to business?" Pablo smirked darkly.

I tried talking but all that came out were muffled noises. Pablo rolled his eyes then took out the gag.

"Why am I here?" I asked him. My voice cracked and tears fell.

"Sugar you're here because I need you. Not only are you close with joey but Elliot. Now both of them have done things to make me angry. You sweet heart are going to make joey and Elliot come to me."

"Please don't hurt them." I begged. "I'll do anything, just don't hurt my Friends."

"Joey is your friend, Elliot is more. I've seen the way you both are together. Now, let's have some fun while we wait shall we."

Joey POV

We all got to LA base when I heard screaming coming from inside. My heart broke as Lauren's cried for help filled my ears.

"Damn she's got some lungs." Emilio laughed a little.

I shot him an evil glare which shut him up immediately. "Go in. I don't care who dies in the process. We get Lauren and leave. No one gets out alive other than us." I demanded.

I got a bunch of nods then we all ran inside. Luckily we didn't have to kill many people. We all separated to look for Lauren.

Me, Abbott, Grayson, Elliot and rose all found her in a room. It was my old room from when we move states. I stayed in that room before Pablo kicked me out.

"Don't you dad fucking move Pablo. Get away from Lauren now." I glared at him.

"Don't do that Joey. I have the upper hand here." Pablo said darkly then stood up, pointing a gun at Lauren's head.

She let out a scream and cried. "Get away from her now." Elliot warned him although I could hear the fear in his voice.

"Anyone makes a move, Lauren dearest dies." Pablo made a banging noise that made rose, Abbott and Grayson jump.

"Pablo be reasonable. She's a teenager, let her live her life. Joey has the money, no one has to die here today." Rose spoke to him.

"Rose Di'Angelo. Nice to see you again beautiful. Where's the family?"

"Right here." Salvatore, Emilio, Jace, Damon, Elijah and Mitch all came into the room.

"Isn't this all to familiar Jace? Remember when my nephew killed your precious Cora?" Pablo smirked.

"Don't you dare speak of Cora. Get away from the girl now." Jace sounded dark and dangerous.

"I don't think so. Maybe I will just pull the trigger." Pablo smirked then it happened.

A gunshot went off. My eyes widened as I looked. Sat in the chair was Lauren. Her head was hanging while her body went limp.

"Dammit." Jace yelled. Elliot was stood there tears streaming down his cheeks as he looked at the body.

"I'll kill you." I leaped at Pablo. I managed to get him on the floor while I laid punch after punch at his head.

"I'll kill you pablo. She didn't deserve this. You're going to pay." I shouted. I heard people moving around me while I kept on hitting Pablo.

I got up and stood above him. I pulled out my hand gun and pulled on him. "You don't get to live anymore. I'll see you in hell Pablo. Make sure you can hide because I will torment you." With that I pulled my trigger.

I looked over my shoulder to see Lauren's body on the floor with Elliot over her. "Wake up. Come on baby come back to me."

Rose was cuddled up to Salvatore while she cried. Jace was muttering to himself while his eyes were glossed over, the same with Elijah.

"Joey?" Abbott called me. I looked over at him to see his eyes red and his teared stained cheeks.

"I'm so sorry. Abbott I'm so sorry." I broke down.

He immediately came over to me and pulled me against his chest. We both cried over the loss of our friend and cousin.

"We have to go tell the others and her parents. I'll get my dad and some men to come get her." Abbott whispered to me.

"No, I messaged Landon and the boys so they should be here soon." I told him.

"Joey?" I heard Landon shout.

"Up here." I called back. Landon, Graham, Mason, Owen, Sebastian, Daniel and Liam all ran into the room.

"Where's Pablo?" Liam asked me. I moved out of the way to show them his dead body.

"Get everyone out of here. Well deal with Pablo and get Lauren and funeral set up." Graham smiled sadly at me.

"Elliot, you've got to let her go now." Jace bent down to him.

"She can't be gone. Lauren can't leave me." Elliot cried.

"I know what it's like, mate. I know exactly what you're going through and I know it's shit. It's so fucking shit that you blame yourself. Trust me El, I understand. But you need to let your brothers take her so it's easier from everyone." Jace put a hand on his shoulder.

"I love you Lauren." Elliot whispered. He leaned down and placed a kiss on her lips then closed her eyes.

"That's it, come on we can go back and wait for the boys to get back and then you can say goodbye." Jace lifted him up and took him back to the cars.

Everyone left the boys to take care of Lauren and Pablo. I knew I should have listened, stay low and don't make any friends. Look where it got me now.

My first ever real friend died because of me. She was so pure and innocent yet Pablo chose her to kill. A girl who was supposed to live until she died of old age, a girl who only made people smile.

Only one small pull of a trigger changed all of it. It's all my fault that Lauren is gone. I could've done more to help her. Everyone should blame me for her death. It should have been me.

I blame myself for Lauren's death.

Chapter 25. The funeral

Song: gone- Katrina Stuart. (Mature content)Joey POV (three weeks later)

"Are you ready?" Abbott put one arm around my waist.

"It's my fault." I whispered.

"Hey, no it's not. Lauren wouldn't want you blaming herself. It's Pablo's fault that she's a dead. Don't beat yourself up."

"I can't help it. I could've done more to help. We waited to long and now Lauren is gone. She should blame me."

"Joey listen to me. I knew Lauren better than she knew herself. She wouldn't want you blaming yourself. Trust me, Lauren wouldn't want that on you."

"How do you know?" I sniffled.

"Because she knows what self blame feels like. Everyday Lauren blamed herself for how her parents acted. No matter how hard I tried to talk her out of it, Lauren still blamed herself. I know what it does to someone and it's shit, no one blames you for what happened, especially Lauren." Abbott hugged me tightly.

"We better go before we're late. Everyone has already left." He added. Abbott laced his fingers through mine and lead me out of the house.

We got into my blue Lamborghini with Abbott driving.

Eventually, we got to the church where Lauren was to be buried. Harriette came up to me when I got out of the car.

"I'm so sorry Harriette." I cried on her shoulder.

"No one blames you joey. We'll all get through this." She squeezed me then let go. "Let's go."

"Here we are to remember Lauren Elizabeth stone. She was a daughter, cousin, friend and loved one..." the guy went on.

Abbott, Grayson, miles, Hendrix, Abbott's dad and Lauren's dad all carried her coffin in and out.

After a few words from close friends and family, it was finally my turn.

"Lauren was the first friend I had ever made. With her bright blue hair and kind eye and soft smile. She accepted me to be her friend when no one else would. I was the weird new girl no one had ever seen before." I began to cry again. "From being new and alone I went to the new girl who managed to be friends with the most popular group at school." I turned to her coffin. "Thank you so much Lauren for being there for me and giving me an amazing friend who I am glad to call sister."

Abbott came up to me and hugged me while I sobbed into his chest. After the coffin was put into the ground, everyone left.

~~~~~~~~~~~~~~~~~~~~~~~~

When I got home, I locked myself in my room. I took off my dress then got in the shower, hoping I would feel better afterwards.

After a few minutes, I felt arms go around my waist. Light kisses were placed on my neck and shoulder.

"Penny for your thoughts." Abbott put his chin on my shoulder.

"Not much. I just feel bad now because you lost your family. If I just listened to pablo and not make friends then you would still have Lauren." I cried.

Abbott turned me around so I my face was in his chest. He held me while I cried as he went through my hair with his fingers.

"If Lauren hadn't of met you then I would of had to see her sad all the time." Abbott told me.

"What do you mean?" I asked.

"Her mom and dad were aggressive drunks. Before you, Lauren barely smiled and then all you had to do was say hello and her face would light up."

"That wasn't me."

"Yes it was. When you gave her money and a car, you don't know how much you helped her. She couldn't stop smiling because it was you who helped her when she needed it most. As a stranger you didn't have to do that yet you still did. Lauren will be forever grateful for that." Abbott smiled softly at me.

"Thank you." I sobbed even more.

"It's what Lauren would have said." I could hear the smile in his voice as he spoke.

"I know it would've. She was a great person." I sniffled.

"Yeah she was. Now let's get some sleep." Abbott picked me up, my legs and arms wrapped around him.

He shut off the water then stepped out. I could feel him wrap a towel around his waist then one around me.

"Can we lay like this for a while?" I asked him.

"What? Naked?" He chuckled. I nodded and he rubbed my back. "Of course. If that's what you want."

Abbott dried me then laid me down. After a few minutes, he climbed under the sheets with me. Our feet were tangled at the end of the bed while we just looked at each other.

"I love you joey."

"I love you Abbott." I smiled a little.

He leaned his head down and pecked my lips. Small pecks turned into a full on make out. He moved so he was hovering over me.

"Let me take your mind off things." He whispered in my ear.

"Please." I moaned a little.

I could already feel Abbott's hard length poking me. He kissed me then entered. There was a small pain but wasn't as bad as the first time.

"You're so gorgeous y'know that?" Abbott smiled.

"Not entirely." I giggled.

"Then let me show you how much I love you and think your beautiful." He smirked then thrusted into me.

Abbott pulled one of my legs over his shoulder so he could go deeper and faster. Our moans and heavy breathing filled the room as Abbott kept slamming into me.

A familiar knot formed in my stomach and I knew I was close.

"Baby I'm close." I breathed out.

"Fuck. So am I." He groaned.

We both climaxed and Abbott fell down beside me.

"Do we have to change the sheets again?" I whined.

"Not this time baby. We can do whatever you want." He replied.

"Good." I giggled then rolled on top of him.

It doesn't take a genius to figure out what we did for the rest of the night.

Chapter 26. Epilogue

Joey POV (five years later)

"Thank you so much miss smith. Here's your pay and I'll see you next week." The man handed me an all to familiar envelope.

"Thank you mr Casey. It's a pleasure doing business with you." I said then walked back to my car.

When I got back to my house, I saw my amazing husband and little girl waiting for me.

"Mommy!" My little girl screamed with a huge smile on her face.

"Hey baby girl. How was kindergarten?" I took her from her dad.

"It was good. I made a new friend. His name is Austin."

"That's good. Lauren why don't you go find uncle Elliot?" I asked her. Yes, I named my daughter after Lauren. It was scary how much my daughter acted like my best friend.

"Ok mommy." Lauren hugged me then ran inside.

"How is my gorgeous wife?"

"Tired. Abbott I want him to come out." I whined.

"Not long now baby." Abbott put his hand on my huge stomach.

"Why do I still go out while I'm like this? I feel like a whale and I waddle." I whined.

"You look sexy like it. It's a real turn on for me really. Anyway, Landon has a surprise for you anyway."

"What is it?" I asked.

"He's in the theatre so you have to go see for yourself." Abbott kissed me then I went inside.

I got inside to see Landon in the theatre room. "Abbott said you have a surprise for me."

"Yes I do. They came a very long way to see you so be grateful Mrs stone. This is the last one until that baby is born." Landon said then left.

"So what is it?" I yelled after him.

"Right here sweet cheeks." A British accent filled my ears.

"Ella." I squealed and hugged her.

"What is it with you brits leaving me for so long at a time?" I laughed.

"You know I've been busy. I've been in New Orleans for a couple weeks. I still can't remember about my past though." She sighed.

"It's alright. I'm just so glad your here." I smiled.

"Yes. And your pregnant again." Ella put her hand on my bump.

"Yep. Got a little boy this time."

"Any names?"

"Yeah. Memphis. My friend from England suggested it." I told her.

"Really? How come I've never met the famous England gang?"

"Because your never here. Speaking of that, I have a couple coming tomorrow."

"Well I'll be hanging around to meet them. But I'm tired so I'll be off to bed. Night darling and look after yourself." Ella hugged me once more then went upstairs. ~~~~~~~~~~~~~~~~~~~~~~~~~~~

"Good morning America." I heard shouting from downstairs.

"Babe can you go see to them. I'll be down in a minute." I nudged Abbott.

"Hmm, yeah." He kissed my cheek then got up.

I got up as well, doing my business then doing downstairs.

Jace, Arorah, Kieran, Mitch, Rose, Elijah, Salvatore, Luna and Damon were all sat in the kitchen.

"Damn girl you're glowing." Luna squealed when she saw me.

"Nice to see you to Luna. I'm so ready for him to come out now." I laughed a little. "Happy birthday jace." I added.

"Thanks. Not really a birthday anymore though." He sighed.

"We know your still miss her. We all do." Rose hugged him.

"Oh jace. My friend is staying here as well so she's actually using your room. Is it ok if you share with one of the boys?" I asked.

"Yeah. Sure, I don't mind. Where is everyone anyway?" Jace replied.

"Everyone is out. They went clubbing last night so they're probably passed out somewhere at the front of the house." I laughed.

"Sounds like them. Anyway, it was good to see you but I have to go see Sam." Ella came in.

"Ok, see you then." I shrugged and she left.

"Damn brits. Always for places to be." Elijah joked and shook his head.

Lightning Source UK Ltd.
Milton Keynes UK
UKHW020752301222
414627UK00014B/797